The Long View

The Long View

Essays, Poems, Stories

Susan Ford Wiltshire

Cordelia Hollis
PUBLISHING

The Long View

Copyright © 2015 by Susan Ford Wiltshire

"Sam Houston and the *Iliad*" first appeared in the *Tennessee Historical Quarterly* 32.3 (Fall, 1973). It is anthologized in *Houston and Crockett: Heroes of Tennessee and Texas*, ed. Herbert L. Harper (Nashville 1986).

A longer version of "Antigone's Disobedience" appears in *Arethusa* 9.1 (Spring, 1976).

"On Authoring and Authority" appears in *Southern Humanities Review* 21.3 (1987).

"Hospitality or Exile: Race, Sexual Orientation, and Sophocles" is included in *American Crisis, Southern Solutions* (NewSouth Press, 2008).

"Liza's Quilt" is anthologized as "The Auction," in *Home Works: A Book of Tennessee Writers*, (University of Tennessee Press, 1996) and as "The Quilt," in *Let's Hear It: Stories by Texas Women Writers* (Texas A&M University Press, 2003).

A note on the spelling of Vergil's name: Vergil's Roman name was Publius Vergilius Maro. For various reasons "Vergil" became corrupted to "Virgil" in the Middle Ages, a spelling now common, especially in British usage.

Editor: Bard Young, bardyoung@bardyoung.com
Editorial assistant: Angela Edwards Smith

ISBN: 978-0-9914907-3-8

Cordelia Hollis Publishing
122 N. Main St.
Dickson, TN 37055

The Long View

Poems

Short Stories

Colonus: A Novella

Penelope Returning

Backstories

Every book has a backstory. This one has several. Rather, the essays have backstories. The poems and stories *are* backstories.

This book is a thank you note for all the books I have been fortunate to read, the wonders I have seen, and the stories I have heard over a lifetime. I have divided the essays into four sections: "Tradition," "Connection," "Equality," and "Home." They are as true as I can make them. As for the poems, short stories, and the novella, they, too, are true, but none of it ever happened.

My first long journey took me from Turkey to Italy before I ever left my third-year Latin classroom in Lubbock, Texas. Over two thousand years ago the Roman poet Vergil wrote his epic the *Aeneid* in the form of Homer's *Iliad* and *Odyssey,* following the hero Aeneas from the fall of Troy to the future site of Rome, together with diversions through North Africa and the Underworld. I was enchanted then and still am.

My interest in the Classical Tradition—the influences of the ancient Greeks and Romans on America—began with an accident, as most passions do. During my first graduate semester at Columbia University, I was wandering lost in the university library looking for the section on the Roman poet Horace when I came upon Lester Cappon's two-volume collection of correspondence between Thomas Jefferson and John Adams in their retirement. I was astonished that these two founders of the American Republic were writing about how to scan a line of Homer, whether Thucydides or Herodotus were the better historian, and what Theognis meant by the term *aristocracy.*

It had never occurred to me that what we know from the past might also inform the present. My curiosity about these influences has lasted a lifetime. The ancient classics are not only charming but useful.

Connection for me has to do mostly with teaching and learning. Eudora Welty said she never became a teacher because she didn't have the patience for it. I do. For me connection is a matter of conversation—with students, with books and ideas, with the larger world in which we live. I knew from the age of eleven I would be a teacher. For a female in my time and place, that meant I would be a high school English teacher.

Then two things happened. On my way out of a professor's office during my freshman year in college, the professor's assistant asked me if I had ever considered teaching in college. No, I replied . . . and then began wondering why not. From that moment I never considered anything else.

The following summer my mother and I went on a long-anticipated trip to Europe. I was eighteen and had never been east of Dallas. We rode a train to New York, embarked on the Greek ship *Olympia*, and sailed all the way to Piraeus, the port city of Athens. I never recovered from that first love affair with Greece. I went back to Austin in the fall, dropped my English major, and began the study of Greek. I already loved Latin. Now I loved Greek too.

After four years of graduate study and a Ph.D. from Columbia, I was ready to start. I even had a job. In those years there were enough college jobs to go around, even for women, and I had my choice of three nice ones. I chose to go to the University of Illinois in Champaign-Urbana.

But there was a problem. I did not know how to teach. I had never taught one college class as a teaching assistant or in any other capacity. Teaching was not highly regarded, maybe not regarded at all, in the high-toned graduate school in which I was "trained."

After the first meeting of my first class and the students had all left the room, Don Deese walked back in. "Miss Ford, I may be wrong, but I wonder if this is the first time you've ever taught?" "How did you know?" I gasped. He said, "I have a book that might help you. I'll bring it next time." Don had been in the Teacher Corps in East Tennessee. Maybe that's how he came upon *Teacher* by Sylvia Ashton-Warner, the book that has been my teacher's guide ever since.

When Ashton-Warner set out to teach five-year old Maori children in her native New Zealand, she was given standard British colonial textbooks for her classroom. Soon she discarded those texts and asked the children to tell stories they had heard at home. She wrote them down and taught the children to read from their own stories.

That's how I learned to begin with what students already know. Then teacher and student embark together, sharing a journey to new lands, books, and ideas. Those journeys will be as different as the students are, because they all start from different places. This means that the teacher too will grow, shift, and change along the way.

Here is an example. For many years I taught a freshman seminar at Vanderbilt in which we read the *Iliad* and the *Odyssey*, a sizable number of Greek plays, and works of the most important philosophers. In his *Ethics*, Aristotle treats the question of whether parents love their children more, or children love their parents more. I had never resolved that question for myself, so one day I asked the students what they thought. Forest Ralph, a freshman from Houston, spoke up from the back of the room. He said, "Parents love their children more than children love their parents, and that's a good thing. Otherwise there would be no progress in the world, because progress requires risk and change, and what parents want most for their children is to be safe." In the same course during a following year, we were discussing the nature of heroism in Homer's *Iliad* when I asked the students to name some of their heroes. Several young men mentioned their fathers. Then, Amanda Smith raised her hand. "My mother is my hero, because she works three jobs so I can come to a school like this."

After that, I asked this class every fall during our discussion of Aristotle what their parents want most for them. The most common answers were "success" or "happiness," in one order or the other. Then I would ask them, "What is the last thing your parents say to you when you leave the house on Friday night in a car?"

As for equality, my sense of and concern for it came from my mother.

When I was in the sixth grade, my mother decided to host a tea party in our home. There were two guests, the principal of my elementary school, Ivy Savage, and Mae Simmons, the principal of a segregated elementary school across town in East Lubbock. Mother had met Mrs. Simmons in one of her volunteer activities and thought the two principals would have much in common and would enjoy meeting each other.

This was in the early fifties and may have been the first integrated social occasion in our town. What I observed that day as we drank tea around our fireplace made an indelible imprint. Mrs. Simmons was charming and poised. Mrs. Savage was visibly agitated and barely spoke. That's when I saw firsthand that something was wrong in our society.

I was in college at the University of Texas in Austin at the height of racial integration activities and soon became active in the campus YMCA/YWCA, where most of the planning and action was originating. Late in my junior year, I was nominated to become president of the YWCA for the following year. That same week the *Dallas Morning News* ran a five-day front-page series on the

"YM(?)A" in Austin. What the question mark meant at that time and place was clear.

Calls started coming in to my mother and even to my grandmother from all over the state about what was going on and why I was involved in these "Communist" activities. I was in so much distress I finally called my mother to ask her what I should do. Her response? "Susan, make up your own mind, and we will support you 100 per cent."

Later, when I got involved in a contentious lawsuit at my university that consumed my attention for three years, my mother said to me, "Everything you have done your whole life has prepared you for this." She also sent me a clipping from the Texas Tech student newspaper in 1925. The story reported that "two members of the fairer sex have asked to practice with the Red Raider Band. They have only asked to practice, but that's the camel's nose under the tent, and soon they will want to march, too." Guess who was one of the two?

In the last decades of her life my mother set forth again. In response to the AIDS crisis she started a monthly meeting in our home of Parents and Friends of Lesbians and Gays for parents of gay children in nearby communities who had no other support. My oldest brother rebuked her for this, saying she was encouraging homosexuality. She responded, "I will live my life according to my conscience, not yours." Later she took on the Methodist bishops for their anti-gay stance. She loved to say, "Sanctified ignorance is still ignorance."

The influence of my mother and many others on how I think was and is formative, but so is geography. *Home,* for the ancient Greeks, was one place above all others: Delphi. Delphi was considered the center of the earth and the most important oracle in the Greek world. To this day, visitors to Delphi see a sign upon entering the town declaring them henceforth to be "citizens of the world." The ancient Stoics, too, thought of human beings as "cosmopolitans," that is, as citizens not of a city or state but of the world. They seemed to think we have retractable roots that can be set down wherever we land. For them it was the life of the mind that counts.

I prefer home in people and places. For me there have been four—two in Texas and two in Tennessee. I was raised in Lubbock and lived there for my first seventeen years. Where I grew up, however, was on our family farm further up on the vast treeless plains of the Texas Panhandle where we lived in the summers. There I had time to read stacks of books a week, learn the long view of things, and think.

Austin was the first green place I ever lived. I loved the environment, the history, the people, the challenges both inside and outside the classroom. After four years at the University of Texas, I was ready to prepare for a similar life. At the end of four years in New York City where we were both graduate students, I met Ashley Wiltshire from Virginia. When we married, we wanted to return to the South to a place where, if we worked very hard, we could make a little bit of difference.

Circumstances brought us to Nashville. Almost immediately we found a neighborhood we cared about, good work to do, friends we cherished, and a church that has stretched and nourished us for decades. Early on, we also bought a farm sixty miles west of Nashville where on the weekends we raised our children, cattle, and a big garden. Green is everywhere, and a lovely stream flows by in front of the house.

These days, I live full time on that farm with the man of my dreams. Ashley and I still raise cattle and enjoy frequent visits with family and friends. The small rural county where our farm is located is named for Sam Houston.

Essays

Tradition

The *Aeneid* for a Lifetime
A poem that changes and grows as we change and grow

A colleague once said he never understood the *Aeneid* until he had a son. But one does not need to have a son to understand the *Aeneid*. It is sufficient to be a son or a daughter. It is sufficient to be or to have lost a parent. It is sufficient to have loved and won— or loved and lost. It is sufficient to care in any way about another person or about the world.

The *Aeneid* is a poem that summons us to bring to it everything we have learned from our lives, our friends and family, and from all the other books we have ever read. We see in it the excruciations of childhood and adolescence, the complications of mature adulthood, and the problems and increasing clarity that come with age—in short, the Age of Ascanius, the Age of Aeneas and Dido, and the Age of Anchises.

The Age of Ascanius

In a way, the *Aeneid* is a poem about children, or at least about one child, Ascanius, whom we first see scrambling with too-short legs to keep up with his father as they flee their besieged and burning city of Troy. We see him next in Carthage in Book 4 as a child eager to go hunting and to experience some of the regular pleasures of childhood, having been for too long the uprooted only child of a loving but depressed and distracted single parent. We see him cross over into a new status as he leads his peers in the equestrian exhibition in Book 5, a rite of passage symbolic of his future leadership in public life. We see him still as an adolescent in

Book 7 as he chatters playfully about eating tables but then as he makes the deadly mistake of shooting Silvia's pet deer—with the connivance of Allecto—the act that starts the war in Italy. Finally we see him in that poignant scene in Book 9, serving as a surrogate general in the absence of his father, offering rewards and making promises to Euryalus that he will honor the latter's mother as his own should Euryalus die on his nighttime sortie with Nisus.

But in another way, the *Aeneid* is a poem *for* children. Children love good stories. Someone said that God created people because God loves a good story. For years I told children stories from the *Odyssey* but reserved the *Aeneid* for adults, at least young adults, with the heavy weight of history that it carries and the profoundly adult conflicts it explores. I learned that I was wrong about that when I spent three days at an Aeneid Institute for elementary teachers. I learned at least three things from the wonderful teachers who participated in that institute: (1) Vergil's stories are compelling even for very young children; (2) we can teach anything to anyone if we ourselves are excited about it; and (3) it is just possible that children are ready for hard stories sooner than we suspect.

We also know that there are several different kinds of giftedness. One of them is moral, and it often appears early in a child. All of us have known some children who command a firmer sense of justice than some adults. By adolescence young people are suspecting that life is fairly untidy after all and that simple conclusions don't come at twenty-eight or fifty-eight minutes after the hour. They begin to know what adults know and what movies and TV don't know—as Walker Percy puts it in *The Thanatos Syndrome*, that "TV has screwed up millions of people with [its] little rounded-off stories. Because that is not the way life is. Life is fits and starts, mostly fits."

It is the child's "Why?" that brings us to the complications of middle age.

The Age of Aeneas and Dido

Most of the wars of adults, like those in Vergil's lifetime, are civil wars. Sam Houston, who loved the classics and was raised by the Cherokees, said: "I have yet to be wronged or deceived by an Indian, but every wound I have ever known was the work of my own blood." At the end of the movie *Platoon*, the character Chris Taylor comes to realize that the war in Vietnam was really a war between the good and evil in ourselves.

The entire *Aeneid* is a walking civil war: between public duty and private desires; between a longing for the past and an obligation for the future; between private passions and work for the world (there are so few to work for the world); and between hospitality toward and aggression against strangers.

Modern hospitality is typically a transaction among friends. Ancient hospitality (and certainly this is true in the *Aeneid*) is a transaction among strangers. Modern hospitality reinforces our familiarities. Ancient hospitality alters us by exposing us to outsiders. When a stranger from the public realm enters one's private space, change occurs in both the host and the guest. In the *Aeneid* these meetings between the public and private realms invariably result in the transformation of both.

Of at least five major episodes of hospitality in the *Aeneid*, the first, between Dido and Aeneas, is the most complex and catastrophic. Considering that episode from the perspective of hospitality may help provide a widened perspective on this drama of adult life that has so fascinated even the young from the time of St. Augustine as a boy to the present.

The relationship between Dido and Aeneas usually evokes the making of judgments. Is Dido hopelessly irrational, a woman

10

who cannot cope with reality? Is she the innocent victim of circumstances beyond her control? Or is she the victim of a man who himself cannot cope with reality? Was it utterly impossible for the two of them to work out their differences in a rational manner?

And what about Aeneas? Is he the innocent victim of a conniving enchantress? Is he responsible for leading her on? Did he collaborate in her assumption that their relationship was a marriage? Why did he not tell her he had decided to leave Carthage? Were a furtive departure and a maddened suicide the only possible outcomes of a great love between two peers in excellence, beauty, power, and wit?

One way to suspend judgments and widen the range of perspectives is to consider the tragedy of Dido and Aeneas in the context of hospitality. Two thresholds separate any man and any woman, that of hospitality and that of eros. In Vergil's epic, the royal queen and the refugee prince step across both of them. Their catastrophe results from the fact that hospitality and eros are protected by conflicting sanctions. Hospitality is a practice of the public realm, eros of the private, and even these two heroic characters cannot handle the competing claims that press upon each of them.

Still, they fell in love. In a sense their love chose them. There is a necessary quality about their coming together, an inevitability that eludes conscious choice. What we would call timing and circumstances and compatibility—and what the ancients called fate—made it certain that they would love each other, just as the other circumstances of their lives made it certain that their love could not last. They had touched each other, and for a season they believed that their love alone could bear the weight of their lives.

The results were disastrous. For Dido the disaster evolved from her assumption of a public status for the personal relationship conceived with Aeneas in the cave during their retreat from the storm. The difference between a love affair and marriage is that one is private and the other is public. Dido's passionate desire was for the one to be the other.

But the disaster arose from the very practice that contributes most to our civility. It is the test of civilization to offer hospitality to strangers, and that is what Dido offered Aeneas. "Extend hospitality," Anna had urged Dido, *indulge hospitio* (4.51). Dido did the humane thing in inviting the homeless Trojans to share in her kingdom. Eros, however, is also part of our humanity. Shortly before she dies, Dido laments, "It was not permitted to me to live my life as a widow free of guilt in the manner of a wild animal and not to experience such cares" (4.550–51). In short, she is saying that it was not permitted to her to be human also in the matter of eros. True, Dido collapsed her public role into her private life and then gambled it all on one other human being, one who was no more or less frail than any of the rest of us. Her tragedy results from the collapse and the gamble, as well as from the fierce pride that left her no honor but death when he left. But her end is also a tragedy born of her enormous humanity—her hospitality and her eros.

For Aeneas the disaster was less acute and more generally diffused in his sadness. For him the public status of marriage with Dido was never acknowledged. "Never did I offer you marriage," Aeneas says to Dido as things fall apart; "never did I enter into such an agreement" (4.338–39). While true that he acted as her consort in the building of her city, he did it not as a past Trojan or future Roman ruler but actually wearing Carthaginian royal garb (4.262–63). He was playing a role, one for which we have no evidence of joy on his part.

Aeneas is like an oldest son who wants very much to be loved and not to hurt anybody. He cannot fight his fate because that would be too dangerous: no protective barrier stands between him and the universe of his adult responsibilities. We know from the text of the *Aeneid* that he loves Dido greatly (cf. 4.395, 6.455)—only the young wonder how Aeneas could love her and leave—but he has a public destiny that does not include his private happiness. Like Edith Wharton's Ethan Frome, he suffers his duty silently and will bear his burden to the end. His suffering, like that of Dido, comes from his great humanity—from his strength, not his weakness.

Wounds as great as these two suffer sometimes bear within them, by some mysterious economy, the eventual sufficiency of their own healing. When Aeneas meets the shade of Dido in the Underworld in Book 6, there is no understanding or forgiveness between them. But something happens that transcends those altered circumstances. In their encounter, Aeneas finally faces Dido's consequences, and perhaps also his own, of loss caused by his leaving. He weeps grievously and is overwhelmed by the great hurt that he now allows himself to feel (6.475). In this knowledge, he is no longer the unknowing shepherd who once had fatally wounded an unsuspecting doe (4.71–72). As for Dido, she has regained her agency over her own choices. Moving to the side of her husband Sychaeus, she is once more in possession of her dignity and identity. She no longer is pitiful, just as Aeneas no longer is insensitive. Their encounter was fateful, but this moment between them oddly redeems part of their loss.

The Age of Anchises

For readers of the *Aeneid* it is sometimes hard to remember that Aeneas's father Anchises is never physically present in the narrative of the poem. He died at Drepanum in Sicily just before Aeneas set out into the storm that would blow him onto the shores of North Africa. We learn about him from Aeneas's tale at the banquet in Carthage, and then we encounter his ghost in the Underworld in Book 6.

That's it.

Yet Anchises is a powerful presence through the epic. In Book 2 of Aeneas's tale at the banquet in Carthage, we learn that Anchises did not want to leave Troy even in its downfall. We human beings often seem hard-wired to resist change, especially the very young and the very old. Anchises says he would be content to die in his own burning home and even to be bereft of a funeral. It takes a sign from the heavens to stir him onward, but it is a sign that he is the first to interpret, perhaps because of his superior experience.

Book 3 records how Anchises makes a serious mistake. When the oracle at Delos urges Aeneas to "seek his ancient mother," Anchises interprets that to mean Crete when in fact it means Italy. For the old to make mistakes is all right. Even to become a ghost is all right. But simply to fade away, to absent oneself from the fate of the next generation is *not* all right. The *Aeneid* is weighted with history because older people who care about the fate of the generations to come populate its pages. Thus, in the third stage as in the first, the *Aeneid* is a poem *about* older people and also *for* older people.

Think for a moment about *Romeo and Juliet* and *West Side Story*. Structurally they are the same story, but one is a story about adult presence, the other about adult absence. The younger generation needs and deserves adult presence. If the choice is one between being overbearing and underbearing, let us not hesitate to be overbearing. Aristotle says that bashfulness is an ornament to the young but a reproach to old age.

The *Aeneid* is a poem for a lifetime because it is about youth, middle, and old age, and for all three of those ages, too. It

14

is a poem that teaches us to cherish the old without becoming old, regardless of our years. It teaches us that no matter how acute our expertise, we will interpret the unknown by analogy. It shows us that it is a true use of literature to help avoid personal repetition of demonic tragedy. It teaches us that the more we know—about the *Aeneid* as well as about life—the more we will honor diversity. Rachel Maddux writes in *The Green Kingdom*: "Knowledge destroys uniformity. To know anything, alive or dead, is to trade its wholeness for a constantly changing variety. Who welcomes this change creates adventure; who retreats from it fears life; who denies it asserts death." (404).

The *Aeneid* does not teach us everything we need to know, but that grand epic poem teaches us a great deal about how to live a life.

Sam Houston and the *Iliad*

More about Sam Houston

Sam Houston was born in Virginia in 1793 and raised in east Tennessee. As a young man he served under Andrew Jackson in the War of 1812, became a lawyer in Nashville, was elected to Congress, and then was elected governor of Tennessee. In time he migrated to Texas, where he led the revolution against Mexico, served as president of the Republic of Texas until statehood in 1845, then was elected senator to the US Congress and finally governor of Texas.

Sam Houston lived a life larger than life because as a boy he fell in love with a book larger than life, the *Iliad* of Homer.

Houston's widowed mother had moved with her children from Rockbridge County, Virginia, to Maryville in East Tennessee. After a brief stint in the local academy and as a clerk in the general store, Sam disappeared one day to live at intervals for three years with Chief Jolly and his Cherokee band on an island where the Hiwassee River merges with the Big Tennessee. In conversations with his earliest biographer, Houston explained his reason.

Having become fascinated with Pope's version of the *Iliad* and other translations from the Greek and Latin, Sam demanded of his teacher that he be taught the ancient languages. When the teacher refused, Sam declared that he would never recite another lesson again, turned on his heels, and left. When his brothers finally found him with the Cherokees, he replied that he "liked the wild liberty of the Red men, better than the tyranny of his own brothers, and if he could not study Latin in the Academy, he could, at least, read a translation from the Greek in the woods, and read it in peace."

When Sam Houston was being mentioned as a possible candidate for the U.S. presidency in 1855 as a Southerner with strong Unionist tendencies, a life was published under the title *The Life of General Sam Houston: The only Authentic Memoir of Him Ever Published.* Charles Lester, who wrote that biography and two others, worked closely with Houston for three months and took much of his material verbatim by dictation.

Lester says that young Houston "devoted all the time he could spare to the studies of a rude frontier school, during which he committed the whole of Pope's translation of the *Iliad* to memory." Lester continues:

No boy ever reads well, till he feels a thirst for intelligence: and no surer indication is needed that this period has come, than to see the mind directed towards those gigantic heroes who rise like specters from the ruins of Greece and Rome, towering high and clear above the darkness and gloom of the Middle Ages. He had, among other works, Pope's *Iliad*, which he read so constantly, we have been assured on the most reliable authority, he could repeat it almost entire from beginning to end.

After describing Houston's school-leaving scene, Lester concludes:

But he had gathered more from the classic world through Pope's *Iliad*, than many a ghostly book-worm, who has read Euripides or Aeschylus among the solemn ruins of the Portico itself. He had caught the "wonted fire" that still "lives in the ashes" of their heroes, and his future life was to furnish the materials of an epic more strange than many a man's, whose name has become immortal.

Houston's intense interest in the *Iliad* also formed a basis for his later oratorical style. George Creel wrote in his 1928 biography:

What saved him from illiteracy were the books that the Virginia pioneers brought with them in their saddle-bags—giving color and delight to the long winter evenings. Pope's "Iliad" came into the boy's possession by loan or gift, and it was this book, as much as any other one thing, that formed his life and pointed his career. The story of the tremendous struggle on the Scamander plain more than ever turned his mind away from peaceful pursuits, casting it in heroic mold, and the sonorous passages gave lasting color to his written and spoken word.

Robert Penn Warren sees in Houston's sojourn with the Indians a consciousness of, among other things, a loss or deprivation, prompted presumably by the family's forced removal from Virginia to Tennessee. Warren writes of Houston:

> We must not think of him as a simple hunter and woodsman, a white runaway gone Indian. His head was full of ambition to read Homer. He carried into the wilderness a copy of Pope's translation of the *Iliad*. If we think of the tall gangly boy, with hunting shirt of red calico and brown hair in a queue down his back, squatting in a thicket, watching the grazing deer or a bear at his bee tree, we must also think of him lying where a stream plunges over gray limestone, and quoting, against the racket of tumbling water, the poetry of that most heroic of all wars. Homer and the wilderness—they gave shape to, and fed, his dream of greatness.

Another biographer attributes Houston's rapid adjustment to and rise in military life to his diligent attention to the *Iliad*. Having been commissioned as an ensign in the U.S. Thirty-ninth Infantry only four months after enlistment in 1813, he was promoted again to third lieutenant only a few months later:

> Houston's rather remarkable adjustment was one of the ways in which the Homer-Pope narrative of the tremendous clash of arms on Scamander plain shaped his life, leading him to

think that he must cast his life in heroic mold. This influence had already affected the way he wrote and spoke; it would become more pronounced as he realized the usefulness of a definite style in living as well as in speaking and writing. Courage on a Homeric scale characterized Houston throughout his life.

The complete reliance on an oral tradition among the Indians with whom Houston passed those years may well have reinforced his interest in memorizing and retaining long passages of the *Iliad*. The Cherokee language was not written down until Sequoyah invented the syllabary for it in 1821, and we know that it was customary in each assembly of the Cherokees to appoint some older man to recite in established form the traditions of the people. Sam also may have put his skills to more immediate use. In his *Memoir* he tells that he had favorites among the Hiwassie girls. They must have been astonished when, according to him, he enlivened their walks through the forest with recitations from the *Iliad*.

Homer does not account for all of Houston's ancient heroes. As president of Texas, Houston likened the Texans at the Alamo to a famous band of earlier warriors: "Leonidas and his Spartans [at the Battle at Thermopylae] never fell more gloriously in Battling for Grecian liberty than the men who perished for Texas." In his first address to Congress he compared Andrew Jackson to Cincinnatus gone back to his plow. Henry Clay became "the Ajax whose battle axe glistened aloft in the thickest of the fight for the Compromise of 1850." During a brief visit to Nashville from Indian country in 1831, Houston with his usual dramatic flair—he had in fact belonged to the Dramatic Club as a young lawyer in Nashville—commissioned a painting of himself as Marius, the Roman consul.

But it was Homer who came first. Houston matured considerably in his later life as a person and as a leader, particularly after his marriage to Margaret Lea in 1843. His vivid imagination never flagged, however, and we can safely assume that his sense of adventure, his willingness to take risks, his grand, sometimes grandiose, perspective of the world were all formed in significant part by his absorption of the *Iliad* at the impressionable age.

Antigone's Disobedience
How I learned I was wrong about Antigone

In both the Hebrew and Greek stories, human history is ushered in by an act of divine disobedience. For the Hebrews, that act was the eating of an apple in the Garden of Eden against the will of God. For the Greeks, it was Prometheus's theft of fire from Olympus for the benefit of humankind against the will of Zeus.

In his play *Antigone*, the Greek playwright Sophocles tells of another profound act of disobedience when Antigone buries her brother in defiance of the edict of Creon, who became the regent of Thebes after the death of Oedipus. As Sophocles tells it, Oedipus was exiled from his city after the discovery that unknowingly he had killed his father and married his mother. After years of wandering as a blind beggar accompanied by his daughter Antigone, Oedipus dies at Colonus, a suburb of Athens. Then his two older sons, Eteocles and Polynices, go to war against each other to gain control of Thebes. They kill each other at the gates of the city, and the regent Creon declares that Polynices cannot be buried since he was the attacker. Following her conscience, Antigone buries her brother anyway.

Great, I thought: Here is an ancient precedent for civil disobedience, the practice that helped Thoreau change history in the nineteenth century; Gandhi, King, and Mandela in the twentieth; and now GLBT people everywhere.

I was wrong. Through a summer of reading about the history of civil disobedience, I figured out why.

Definitions of civil disobedience vary, but in general they include the following points. (1) A law higher than the laws of the land exists, whether it is called conscience or by some other name.

(2) One is obligated to obey the law of the land, if he sees himself as an integral part of society and has a basic belief in social order. (3) On those occasions, however, when the state's laws come into conflict with the "higher law," one's duty requires disobedience of the law of the land. (4) One's objective in disobeying the law is to bring about social or political change; a visible, public protest is therefore required. (5) In breaking the state's law, one must be willing to suffer the consequent punishment; but finally, (6) such punishment will have positive results, because it will help to educate others to the existing evil and will cause others to join in the protest.

Antigone's disobedience to Creon's edict differs from this traditional formulation in three ways, based on three fundamental aspects of her character: her isolation, her apolitical nature, and her autonomy.

First of all, Antigone is utterly isolated from any sort of social involvement. She moves in a "terrifying vacuum" with no hope, perhaps no desire, for help from any source. After the first chilling scene of the play she is isolated from her sister Ismene, whose very existence she later completely ignores. She is isolated from the Theban citizenry, represented by the chorus, whose response to her act is never more than ambiguous at best. She is told further by Creon that she alone of the citizens of Thebes sees things as she does.

She is also isolated as a woman in a man's world. She is isolated from her fiancé Haemon, the son of Creon. Not only is she alone in the dramatic moment, but she cannot even conceive of a precedent in history justifying her intentions. Although she does eventually bring forward one precedent of an abandoned female, that of the suffering of Niobe who lost all her children in a single night, she does so but once, and that only after her own fate has been sealed. Finally, she is isolated even in the manner of her death, as she "alone among mortals will go living to Hades."

Even though a person involved in an act of civil disobedience may often experience solitude in the process of the act itself or in fasting, prison, or exile, that person nevertheless typically feels a strong sense of solidarity with others committed to the same objectives. Antigone, however, is one whose actions increasingly isolate her in both living and dying.

A second difference is that Antigone is *apolis*, to use the word of the chorus. She is a woman without a city, apolitical in the strange world Sophocles has created for her, suspended between the family loyalty of the earlier archaic age and the polis loyalty of fifth-century Athens. She has none of the "city-organizing dispositions" to which the chorus attributes the powers of mankind. The polis is, for the fifth-century Athens, more than just a city or city-state; it is the historical place where history happens. But Antigone operates outside of history, outside of the city. In the end she will be an alien in the lands both of the living and the dead.

If Antigone's were a case of civil disobedience, she would have calculated her actions in such a way as to bring about political change in the city or at least so as to cause Creon to rescind his decree. But Antigone's act is not a means toward such ends. And, unlike the typical civil disobedient, she does not claim from the city even the right to dissent. Bernard Knox points out that on the particular issue on which Antigone defied the city she was right, as the last scenes of the play make clear. The exposure of the corpse of Polyneices is not the interest of the city. But this is accidental to her motives: "Her attitude," he says, "is not that higher, enlightened loyalty to the polis which pursues the best policy rather than the immediately expedient: it is an attitude which ignores the interest of the polis completely."

Which laws may rightly be disobeyed? Some argue that there is never justification for disobeying any law that is not itself target of protest. Others maintain that in the more pervasive issues such as war, racism, and poverty, which normally are not positively condoned by specific laws, one must choose a related law for symbolic protest.

Antigone's fundamental apoliticism contrasts sharply with the political nature of most of the other characters of the play. It is first of all her lover Haemon, the "democrat" and "liberal," who is the political activist of the drama. Haemon, not Antigone, assesses the political realities of the situation as he calculates his approach to Creon, seeking first to win him over by an act of humble filial obedience until it becomes clear that such an approach will not work. The guard, whose function in the play is much more complex than that of mere comic relief, is also political in his own debased way, representing, perhaps, the lowest common denominator of the values of self-preservation that dominate Creon's scale of priorities. Strangely enough, even Ismene is political in that she gauges her responses first on their probable political consequences rather than on their intrinsic merit.

So Antigone's is not the political virtue of a leading citizen such as Pericles, but the isolated, individualistic excellence of an Achilles or an Odysseus. Their ultimate allegiance is to the gods or goods of another order. Antigone is no woman of the city. She is not civil. She is, in short, not polite.

Finally, Antigone is excluded from the traditional definition of civil disobedience by her autonomy, for not only is she outside the bounds of the city; she is also outside law itself. When the chorus calls her "autonomous," it is recognizing not only her independence and self-determination, but also that in becoming a "law unto herself" she has removed herself from all man-made laws. The chorus reflects further its perception of

Antigone's self-will when it declares that her "self-determined temper" has destroyed her. Creon knows that this independence is no quirk of the moment for Antigone, as he indicates when he observes that of the two sisters, Ismene became "mindless" just now, while Antigone was born that way.

There is a kind of autonomy that does not yield to persuasion, including its usual forms of appeal to reason or to the passing of time. In this one respect Antigone does prefigure the experience of later practitioners of civil disobedience. Ismene for instance, tries to appeal to Antigone's reason in order to effect a reversal in her decision. It is this appeal to common sense that is made most often to those bent on a course of civil disobedience— an appeal likewise coming most often from one's family and friends rather than from enemies or strangers. But Antigone is not to be persuaded. Others argue that if reason does not dissuade one from rash actions, then the passing of time will. Creon says that in her tomb Antigone either will die or will learn, though late, and that it is "lost labor to honor those in Hades." Antigone does not learn the error of her ways, either through reason or the passing of time. Instead, she chooses death by her own hands.

The autonomy of Antigone's nature is forcibly underscored by the fact that she is a woman. To the extent that Sophocles wrote *Antigone* as an expression of his interest in the problem of how states should be run, to that extent Sophocles may purposely have chosen a contest in which the antagonist would be a woman. Sophocles himself emphasizes this repeatedly. On at least five occasions Creon displays an almost morbid obsession with being outdone by a woman or being made out to be one himself—once in a speech to the chorus, once to Antigone, three times in the encounter with his nephew Haemon.

If Sophocles had wanted to write a problem play on the meaning of patriotism, then, he would better have chosen two men as antagonists, between whom the contest would have been one of will, of relative strength between peers. "Better to fall, if fall one must, at the hands of a man," Creon himself admits. But with a woman as antagonist, Sophocles creates even more dramatically what would have been to a fifth-century Athenian audience a conflict between two entirely different levels of being, two totally non-contiguous systems of ethics, intentionality, and perception. Antigone says her nature is to join in loving, not in hating, and that she is obeying higher laws than the laws of man.

Antigone's ethic is one of faith over calculation, of love over expediency. She is not the civil disobedient, carefully choosing the moment or context of her disobedience and calculating how she can help change society by her action. In fact, we might say that her act is not one of disobedience at all but, in the most elemental sense of the word, one of defiance—a resounding declaration of "no faith" in Creon's entire system of values.

Antigone's act of burying her brother, then, cannot be termed civilly disobedient. Her isolation, her apoliticism, and the autonomy of her nature all mean that she is far removed from what is essentially a civic tradition meant to change the politics of a society.

But if Antigone's act is not one of civil disobedience, what is it? She herself in lines 400–450 states her motivation clearly in a speech to Creon: that she was obeying divine, unwritten laws higher than those of Zeus or mortals.

Elizabeth Wyckoff translates those lines as follows:
For me it was not Zeus who made that order.
Nor did that Justice who lives with the gods below
mark out such laws to hold among mankind.
Nor did I think your orders were so strong
that you, a mortal man, could over-run
the gods' unwritten and unfailing laws.

That is why some people who choose to go to jail when convicted of an act of civil disobedience say it feels like choosing to go to church.

Socrates as Soldier
A Talk at Texas A&M University

Socrates lived in Athens in the fifth century BCE, over twenty-five hundred years ago. Socrates' life and thought, however, speak directly, right now, to the values of honor, courage, and commitment inculcated at this university. All three values are required for leadership. How Socrates lived—and especially how he died—helps us make distinctions as well as connections among these three values. His example can help us think about these enduring values in new ways.

First, I will review Socrates' résumé, the pertinent facts as we know them. Second, I will comment on the nature of Socrates' leadership, including his military leadership, and suggest what kind of leader he was and why he was so effective. Finally, I will suggest three strategies we can adopt from his example to help us maintain our priorities in both leadership and life.

I

On the face of it, it is hard to imagine that Socrates would ever have even been admitted to Texas A&M University—and certainly not to its Corps of Cadets. He surely would have scored high on his SATs. He knew a great deal about natural science, and his verbal and literary skills were legendary. But he was no physical specimen. By his own admission he had "a stomach rather too large for convenience" (Xenophon, *Symposium* 2.18). He had bulging eyes that he said gave him the ability to see farther to the side than most people (Xenophon, *Symposium* 5.5). Some people said Socrates looked like a satyr—a forest and mountain creature who was a merry, drunken, and lustful devotee of Dionysos, the god of wine and creativity.

Socrates was definitely not squared away. He did not shower often, and if he owned Midnights he never wore them, only one old coat. Forget about the senior boots; Socrates preferred going barefoot. Even if he got into Texas A&M, he surely would not have made it through fish year because he had an odd way of choosing which rules to follow. He tended to listen to an inner voice that he called a *daimon,* some sort of divine sign. I do not know what Socrates meant by that—no one does—but probably he considered it a cross between divine guidance and informed instinct. Perhaps it was close to what we call conscience, but it was deeply rooted in intelligence and common sense.

Of such a character we might not expect much of a military career, certainly not a distinguished one. Surprisingly, Socrates was a superb solider. When he was already thirty-eight years old, a great war broke out between Athens and its archrival Greek city-state Sparta, a contest we know as the Peloponnesian War. Socrates took active part in three major campaigns of the Peloponnesian War. At the Battle of Delium in 424 BCE, the Athenians were defeated, but, thanks to Socrates and others, the retreat was successful. After the battle Socrates' commander, General Laches, wrote the following battle report on Socrates: "I was with him in the retreat, and if everyone were like Socrates, our city would never have come to disaster" (Plato, *Laches* 181b). According to later writers, Socrates saved the lives of some of those retreating with him by following his "divine sign" and insisting on taking a route different from that proposed by others (Plutarch, *Socrates* 591e and Cicero, *Divinatio* 1.54.123). One of his friends reported that Socrates saved his life when he was wounded and no one else would stop to rescue him (Plato, *Symposium* 220–221).

Among the many stories of heroism recounted in Henry C. Dethloff's *Texas Aggies Go to War* (2006), one in particular recalls Socrates' courage and leadership. Captain William C. Hearn (A&M class of '63) assumed command of Bravo Company, First Battalion, Second Infantry of the First Infantry Division only days after arriving in Vietnam in August, 1967. In a fierce firefight on the Cambodian border during the night of December 7, Hearn loaded injured soldiers into a medevac helicopter in a clearing unprotected from incoming fire. The citation for the Silver Star awarded to Hearn reads that he "with complete disregard for his own safety exposed himself to hostile fire" (283–85).

But there is more. Hearn reports that the most harrowing challenge that night was the decision of the artillery to fire "beehive rounds" onto the waves of incoming attackers. This put Hearn's men in grave danger if they were not warned to take cover. Because some of the bunkers did not have radios, Hearn ran under fire to each bunker to spread the word. He explains that in spite of his exposure moving from bunker to bunker to warn his men, he was in less danger than they would have been if left ignorant of the threat. Socrates' *daimon* and Hearn's conscious instincts both saved lives. Finally, somehow it seems not surprising that, like Socrates after his battles, Bill Hearn spent the rest of his career after Vietnam teaching the young. In early 2008 Hearn retired after thirty-three years as the senior student affairs officer at Texas A&M University-Galveston.

We also have stories, from Plato and others, about Socrates' physical hardiness. One who had served with him during a freezing winter campaign far to the north tells how Socrates would walk barefoot on the ice in the bitter cold, wearing only his same old cloak. The regular army guys hated him for this because they were such wimps that they had to bundle up in cloaks and heavy boots (Plato, *Symposium* 220b). On another occasion during a lull in summer operations, Socrates started thinking about something so hard one morning that he stood fixed in the same spot all day. He kept thinking. Midday came. People started noticing. Finally that evening, people brought their pallets out for the night to watch him to see if he moved. He did not. When dawn came, he simply greeted the sun and went on about his business. He had stood in one place thinking about his subject for twenty-four hours. Socrates was tough. He was a good fighter. And he sure did like to think.

Another legendary feature of Socrates' hardiness, not necessarily to be recommended, is that apparently he could drink everybody else under the table, and then walk happily away to start his day's work. We have it on good authority that nobody ever saw him drunk or hung over (Plato, *Symposium* 220a).

This is the military record as we know it. Somehow his military record makes me trust Socrates more, given what happened at the end of his life. This is not simply because he was a veteran. In Latin, to be a "veteran" means only that you're old. But when Socrates later faced a choice between his own life and death, we know that his decision was seasoned by the experience of life or death in battle that most professors and thinkers have not known firsthand.

Socrates' first mission was always teaching and learning. These activities do not sound particularly threatening to a society under normal conditions, especially in a generally beloved if somewhat unusual character with many high-placed friends. But conditions in Athens in 399 BCE were not normal. The Spartans had defeated the Athenians and imposed a junta of thirty Athenian collaborators, including relatives of some of Socrates' friends, to rule the city. Shortly after that, the Thirty Tyrants were overthrown and a very unstable democracy was restored. In this chaotic atmosphere of post 9/11-like turmoil and fear, certain aggrieved parties wanted a scapegoat, and they settled on Socrates. He was indicted on two trumped-up charges of subversion: (1) that he did not believe in the traditional gods but had imported new gods, and (2) that he had corrupted the youth of the city. In his trial he denies that he was irreligious in any way, and that in fact he was very religious because he was teaching about deeply religious things. Maybe some of the youth did learn to disagree with their fathers about such things as politics and whether or not it's important to make lots of money.

Usually such charges would not be cause for capital punishment. This time they were.

Before his execution Socrates was kept for thirty days in prison, where he was often visited by his friends. Clearly, his friends could have paid a fine or a bribe to get him out. In that case Socrates would have had to leave Athens or, if he had been allowed to stay, he would have had to agree to remain silent. Socrates refused such plea-bargaining. He insisted that he would never leave the city that had raised him, even though it had turned on him, and that he would never hold silent in order to remain there.

It was in this period of his trial and impending death that the qualities of honor, courage, and commitment Socrates had nurtured all his life coalesced into a kind of leadership the world had never seen before. Socrates demonstrated that not just personal acts of military courage on the battlefield but also civic values of how to live a life and how to make a community better were worth living and dying for. Socrates always asked basically one question: "What does it mean to live a good life?"

II

What kind of leader, then, was Socrates? First, he was an unconstituted leader. Leaders in military and civilian life are generally constituted—by rank, appointment, or election. Even though he served on juries, as any Athenian citizen would, Socrates never in his life held an elected or appointed office. Like other unconstituted leaders such as Mahatma Gandhi or Martin Luther King Jr., Socrates changed the world not by holding office but by changing the lives of the people around him.

Socrates' idea of education was pretty simple: Spend all the time you can talking about important things with your friends. Socrates loved to ask questions. Usually a single answer to one of his questions was not enough. "But what do you mean by that?" he would counter. And again, "But what do you mean by that?" This often frustrated those engaging Socrates, of course, and it was especially frustrating to the elders of Athens when Socrates' young friends tried it out on them. The questions Socrates asked were not trivial, but the large ones of our lives: What is virtue? What is bravery? What does it mean to be pious or religious? How important is money? Can goodness be taught? For that matter, can leadership be taught?

Socrates denied that he ever taught anything. He maintained instead that what we need to know is already in us. Those around him, sometimes it seemed almost by osmosis, often said they felt they had become better persons simply by being in his company.

We must never underestimate the appeal of simple answers to complex problems. Certitude is far easier than complexity. Simple answers to complex problems, however, are always wrong. Anything we learn and put into practice will necessarily be informed by our own temperament, training, knowledge, and experience. Even in the military, no one size ever fits all. The modern Greek poet George Sefiris observed, "How hard to collect the thousand fragments of each and every soul." Socrates had too much respect for the complexity of life to resort to easy answers.

At the same time, he was not a lazy or careless relativist. He was absolutely committed to the importance of trying to find good answers to hard questions. Here's how he put it:

> I would not be confident in everything I say, but one thing I would fight for to the end, both in words and deed if I were able—that if we believed that we must try to find out what is not known, we should be better and braver and less idle than if we believed that what we do not know it is impossible to find out and that we need not even try. (Plato, *Meno* 86b-c)

The British philosopher Alfred North Whitehead said that "the art of free society consists, first, in maintenance of the symbolic code; and, secondly, in fearlessness of revision. . . . Those societies which cannot combine reverence for their symbols with freedom of revision must ultimately decay." Honor has to do with maintaining the codes that a society has developed, such as the importance of loyalty and telling the truth. Honor is a decision one makes in private, because one can violate the values of loyalty and truth all by oneself. Socrates upheld his own sense of honor when he sought the truth, fought for his city, and refused to escape from its punishments.

Revision of these symbolic codes of honor, however, requires a different virtue, that virtue of courage. Courage is public. This is the courage Socrates had when he held, against the received codes of his society, that qualified women can as effectively serve as leaders of the city as qualified men—and accordingly they should have the same military training and education as men (Plato, *Republic* 451c–452b). He even made a joke about it. He said that to believe otherwise was like saying that bald men and men with long hair have different natures and that therefore one of those two groups can be cobblers but the others cannot (Plato, *Republic* 454c). But Socrates is not just joking; he must really have believed that women can fight, because Aristotle took pains in the next

34

generation to argue that Socrates was wrong on this point (Aristotle, *Politics* 1260b).

I propose, therefore this distinction: One can have a sense of honor or a capacity for courage without the other, and one can be either or both without being a leader. Honor has to do with maintaining traditions, courage with changing them when necessary—and knowing when that is. Honor means doing the expected thing. Courage means doing the right thing for the situation, whether it is expected or not.

Commitment has to do with deciding where to place our honor and our courage. It means choosing where to take our stand, discerning what is uniquely in us to do and to be and where and with whom and for what purpose. Socrates' commitment was to make lives well and the city better. Socrates honored tradition, had the courage to bring about change, and was firm in his commitment to the well-being of the larger community.

Because of this combination, Socrates was an effective leader. He enabled others to think, live, and work together in new ways. Leadership therefore has to do with public life, with gathering others around, and with enabling others out of their new understandings to be who they really are inside—and from that, to move outward to work for the common good. To be a good person, he would say, is to be also a good citizen.

Socrates was not a saint or a super-religious individual honing his private piety or gunning for promotion. Those who gathered around him formed a school after his death, and later their students formed other schools, often with competing ideas but each of them claiming Socrates as model and founder. In the honor and courage of Socrates' last days, they witnessed a new kind of heroism, one they had not seen before—the heroism of someone who was willing to die for his country, not just in warfare but for the sake of the ideas that would make it a better place.

A successful leader is one who has learned to deal with stress in a controlled, measured manner. Socrates fits that description. In what must have been the most stressful moment of his life, when a jury of 501 of his neighbors, friends, and fellow citizens had just voted that he be executed, he did not weep, did not beg, did not parade his wife and children before the court (though he mentioned that option in dismissing it). He just kept on teaching as he had all his life. In fact, he asked his condemners to become teachers themselves. Here is what he said:

> No evil can come to a good man either living or dead. . . . that is why my signal, my daimon, did not warn me off, and why I am not at all angry with those who condemned me or with my accusers. . . . However, one thing I ask them: Punish my sons, gentlemen, when they grow up; give them this same pain I gave you, if you think they care for money or anything else before virtue; and if they have the reputation of being something when they are nothing, reproach them, as I reproach you, that they do not care for what they should, and think they are something when they are worth nothing. And if you do this, we shall have been justly dealt with by you, both I and my sons. (Plato, *Apology* 41)

III

I promised to identify three strategies from the life of Socrates, three habits of mind and heart that can help us keep our heads on straight when we feel overwhelmed by conflict, confusion, or uncertainty.

The first is a sense of humor, which I mean in both the usual and in the broader sense. Capital punishment in classical Athens was carried out by lethal ingestion, that is, by drinking poisonous hemlock. When Socrates' time came, a young prison guard entered his cell with the fateful cup. While Socrates' friends were desperate with grief, Socrates chatted with his young warden, asking him how the poison worked. Then he must have grinned as he kidded the young man with the question of whether the cup held enough of the beverage to pour a little libation to the gods before he went. "Oh no," replied the fellow in horror. "We grind up just enough to kill you" (Plato, *Phaedo* 117b). Here was a man so at peace with himself that he could joke with his executioner.

A sense of humor is not necessarily limited to jokes with one's executioner. And it usually does not mean pranks. It simply means that we do not take ourselves or our circumstances with such absolute seriousness that our liveliness gets blotted out. Humor is like ball bearings, reducing the friction between ourselves and our stress. Music can induce that same sense of ease for some people, and so can poetry.

The second corrective for our perspective is a sense of community—with our family members when we can and with good friends always. By friends I mean not just those who are fun to be with or who can be useful to us in some way, but friends in what Aristotle calls the best kind of friendship: two good people, alike in virtue, helping each other become better (Aristotle, *Nicomachean Ethics* 8.1156b). These are the friends we trust absolutely. These are those who keep the garden green, who may someday save our skin or, more likely, the quality of our lives. An old friend out in the country offered two words of advice: Choose your friends wisely, and choose your mate wisely. Socrates cared for his friends in just this way. His last words before he died were, "Offer a cock to Asclepius" (the god of healing)—apparently on behalf of his dear friend Plato, who was so ill he could not be present at the death.

The third strategy is a sense of history. A sense of history helps us to know we are not alone, that there is someone back there, in our own personal story or in the stories our culture has saved for us, someone whose example helps us to know what we need to do.

This was the case with Socrates during his trial when, surprisingly, he compared himself with Achilles, the brilliant and selfish hero on the Greek side of the Trojan War, who nevertheless chose death before dishonor just as Socrates was doing (Plato, *Apology* 28c-d).

During a hard time in my own life I remembered hearing from my grandfather how his father, my great-grandfather, as a little boy had walked to Texas from Georgia behind a covered wagon with his family after the Civil War. He wore a flour sack for clothes, with holes cut out for his head and arms. In my hard time I kept thinking, "If my great-grandfather could walk from Georgia to Texas, I can finish this dissertation."

The courage we've earned from what we've endured—and what those ahead of us have endured—can help to carry us through.

So, there they are: a sense of humor, a sense of community, and a sense of history—all in the service of honor, courage, and commitment.

Predictably, Socrates made friends with his jailers at the end. When the sacred ship had returned from Delos and the time for the execution arrived, one of the jailers said to him: "To you, Socrates, whom I know to be the noblest and gentlest and best of all who ever came to this place . . . I am sure you will not be angry with me; for others, as you are aware, and not I, are to blame. And so fare well, and try to bear lightly what must be." The jailer burst into tears. Socrates looked at him and said, "I return your good wishes, and will do as you bid." Then turning to his friends he said, "How charming the man is; since I have been in prison he has always been coming to see me, and at times he would talk to me, and be as good to me as could be, and now see how generously he sorrows on my account" (Plato, *Phaedo* 117c-d).

The poison came, Socrates made his last joke about pouring out a little for the gods, instructed his friends to take care of each other, and died. Someone who was there reported to someone who was not: "This was the end of our comrade, a man, as we would say of all then living we had ever met, the noblest and the wisest and most just" (Plato, *Phaedo* 118a).

I would amend that to say that the death of Socrates was not the end but the beginning of a new way to live one's life—a life of honor, courage, and commitment to the common good. Socrates gave all of us who come later the most precious gift of all, the gift of hope—that we can make the world around us better than it was and ourselves better than we were.

In Praise of Inefficiency
The Greek Origins of Public Life and Constitutional Separation of Powers

The ancient Athenians invented the idea that ordinary people can participate in civic life and determine public policy. Aristotle summarizes the Greek belief when he says that human beings are political creatures, that is, that we are fully human only when we live an active public life together with other human beings. In fact, the Greek word for someone who does not participate in politics is *idiotes* or "idiot."

During the Peloponnesian War between Athens and Sparta in the fifth century BCE, the great leader Pericles contrasted the Athenian commitment to public life with the civic inaction of the Spartans. "The Spartans rarely meet in public assembly," he said, "and when they do, they devote only a short time to matters of common concern and much more to what directly affects their own households. They simply assume that while individuals take care of their own affairs, others will attend to public matters. The threats to their common life thus escape unnoticed." In another speech he reminded the Athenians that, unlike the Spartans, they must "banish private concerns and commit themselves instead to the safety of the public realm."

The practice of public participation is therefore a central legacy from ancient Athens to civic life in America. The Greeks also developed another idea that influenced the U.S. Constitution more than any other notion from antiquity: separation of powers.

Certain Greek political theorists proposed that government works best when powers are separated, balanced

40

among competing interests, and kept in equilibrium by checks and balances. The constitutional framers knew that limits on the exercise of power were crucial to the new institutions they were creating.

For the Greeks, mixed government results from the understanding that elements of monarchy, aristocracy, and democracy are all required if a political order is to be stable and harmonious. The notion here is that opposite forces should coexist within the same government to prevent their clash outside it. This theory is as old as the Pythagoreans in the sixth century BCE and was developed further by Plato, Aristotle, and Polybius. It is a class-oriented theory, which posed some problems for the ancients and many more for the American framers, but it takes seriously the truth that conflicting interests do exist in every society and must be taken into account.

The American notion of separation of powers has to do not with conflicting interests but rather with the separate functions of government. Traditionally, these are three in number: the legislative, the executive, and the judicial branches. The notion of checks and balances is closely connected with the first two and could not exist without the presence of mixed government, the separation of powers, or both. Checks and balances serve as a "control mechanism" to prevent one interest group or one branch of government from increasing its power at the expense of the others. In the Constitutional Convention of 1787, the framers constructed a document that combined all three theories.

The earliest origins of these ideas may be traced to the ancient Pythagoreans, that strange and brilliant band of Greek thinkers living in southern Italy in the sixth century BCE who were later to have such a profound influence upon Plato. The sixth century BCE was marked by major social changes, in some ways not unlike those of the eighteenth-century America: colonization, monetary innovations, unprecedented mobility, rationalism in science, and the overthrow of monarchies by the people.

Pythagoras and his followers believed that antithetical forces exist on a cosmic level, but that instead of pulling apart, the tension between them keeps the universe in balance. They understood this harmony as a mathematical equation and saw it in everything—music, medicine, mathematics, and politics. Fragments attributed to the fourth-century BCE Pythagorean Archytas distinguish three forms of government: democratic, oligarchic, and aristocratic. Archytas worked out a mathematical relationship among the three in proportions that will create the most stable order. His emphasis is on stability rather than justice, but it was this idea of mathematical mixture and balance that kindled Plato's imagination.

In one of his latest writings, the *Laws*, Plato argues that just as the increase of one power comes at the expense of others in the sails of ships, in the food of the body, or in the psychological controls of the soul, so also in the operation of governments. If one power increases disproportionately, the government will be destroyed. Plato was the first to think and write in a sustained way about balanced government, but his student Aristotle developed the subject much further. Aristotle disagreed with Plato's tilt toward oligarchy, and his emphases were different, but he too sought a balanced constitution as the solution for the dangerous concentration of political power.

In the *Politics*, Aristotle wrote, "The better, and the more equitable, the mixture in a 'polity', the more durable it will be." In the same passage he expressed his belief that the greater danger to stability comes from the wealthy than from the common people: "It is here that an error is often made by those who desire to establish aristocratic constitutions. [Forgetting the claims of equity], they not only give more power to the well-to-do, but they also deceive the people [by fobbing them off with sham rights]. Illusory benefits must always produce real evils in the long run; and the encroachments made by the rich [under cover of such devices] are more destructive to a constitution than those of the people."

Taking economic issues more seriously than Plato, Aristotle recognized the need for a large middle class to act as a stabilizing influence. He concluded that the best form of political society is one in which power is vested in the middle class and in which good government depends on a large middle class with moderate but adequate property. For Aristotle the stability of the state has an ethical purpose, leading ultimately to the moral betterment of its citizens and to a truly good life.

After Aristotle the most extensive arguments concerning mixed government were tendered by Polybius, the Greek historian of the Roman Republic, in the sixth book of his *Histories*. Polybius attributed Rome's greatness to its mixed constitution. He saw the powers of the consuls, the senate, and the people as interdependent, with each providing checks on the powers of the other two at the same time. The power of the consuls, he said, made the Roman government seem monarchical; the power of the senate, aristocratic; and the power of the people, democratic. No better political system than this can be imagined, he concluded, because "every part remains in its established position, partly because from the beginning, it fears the reaction of the others."

Polybius's main contribution in his assessment of the Roman constitution was to extend the theory of mixed government into a theory of checks and balances whereby each unit of government provides an institutional check upon the others. His belief was not so much that each unit represents a different class, or that a division of labor is simply more efficient, but rather that a system of checks and balances is essential if arbitrary rule is to be avoided.

The remaining question for us, of course, is what did the framers know about all this? Or, perhaps, how *much* did they know and *how* did they know it? James Madison had studied deeply the ancient authorities, and many of the delegates referred to a lengthy study by John Adams on the origins of constitutional government. Alexander Hamilton, in a speech to the Constitutional Convention on June 18, 1781, cited Aristotle together with Cicero and Montesquieu as corroborating his views on the proper mixture of oligarchy and democracy.

Hamilton had written earlier in the *Federalist Papers* of the importance of governmental separation of powers:

> The regular distribution of power into distinct departments; the introduction of legislative balances and checks; the institution of courts composed of judges holding their offices during good behavior; the representation of the people in the legislature by deputies of their own election . . . . They are means, and powerful means, by which the excellences of republican government may be retained and its imperfections lessened or avoided. (Hamilton, *Federalist* 9 [1787]

The issue of the separation of powers is as pressing in our current political life as it was when the Constitution was framed. The executive branch and the Congress are frequently frustrated with each other, and citizens are frequently frustrated with both. The courts are often frustrating to everybody. It is a messy business. Our system of government, however, and our public safety depend on these inefficiencies embedded in the U.S. Constitution.

Rome on the Potomac
Vergil Crossing the Atlantic

Shortly before it adjourned on July 4, 1776, the Continental Congress passed the following resolution: "Resolved: that Dr. Franklin, Mr. J. Adams and Mr. Jefferson, be a committee, to bring in a device for a seal for the United States of America." From the beginning, Americans have understood the importance of symbols for expressing the abstract principles upon which their nation was founded. Some of those images have been visual, some literary. All have called upon the past to validate the present endeavor in the New World. With surprising frequency, the Roman poet Vergil, who died in 19 BCE, has been summoned to speak symbolically for the American experience as well.

The seal commissioned by the Congress required two more committees and the assistance of several consultants before it was finally approved on June 20, 1782. One consequence of the final design was that three quotations from Vergil change hands every time a one-dollar bill is exchanged. All three quotations appear on the back of the one-dollar bill in the representations of the face and the reverse of what is known officially as the Great Seal of the United States.

The Great Seal includes four elements suggested by the original committee: the shield and the motto E PLURIBUS UNUM on the obverse, and, on the reverse, the Eye of Providence and the date of U.S. Independence in Roman numerals, MDCCLXXVI (on the lowest step of the pyramid). The design presented by the third committee to Secretary of the Continental Congress Charles Thomson, on June 13, 1782, included the motto DEO FAVENTE over the unfinished thirteen-step pyramid on the reverse, with the word PERENNIS inscribed below. Thomson, a former Latin teacher in Philadelphia, substituted the Vergilian phrases ANNUIT COEPTIS and NOVUS ORDO SECLORUM above and below the pyramid.

The obverse of the Great Seal is the more familiar. The thirteen stripes or pales on the shield, as well as the thirteen stars in the constellation above the eagle, represent the original colonies. The eagle, symbolic bird of Zeus/Jupiter in Greece and Rome and carried by Roman armies as a sign of their strength and power, holds the olive branch of peace in its right talon and the arrows of war in its left. It faces its own right, that is, toward the olive branch. The motto E PLURIBUS UNUM, "out of many, one," on the ribbon in the eagle's beak alludes to the union of several states in compact with one another, with the executive, and with Congress.

On the reverse, sometimes considered the "spiritual" side of the seal, the inscription NOVUS ORDO SECLORUM, "a new order of the ages," is adapted from Vergil's *Eclogue* 4.5: *magnus ab integro saeclorum nascitur ordo* ("a great order of the ages is born anew"). The Vergilian expression in *Eclogue* 4 of high hopes for a peaceful new age matched well the hopes held by the founders. The divine favor upon the enterprise implied in ANNUIT COEPTIS, "he has nodded approval on our beginnings," is adapted from *Georgics* 1.40, a phrase occurring also at *Aeneid* 9.625: *audacibus adnue coeptis*, "nod approval on our brave beginnings."

This identification of the American experience with the Roman predates the Revolutionary War. In William Strachey's account of the English voyage of discovery to Virginia in 1609, Captain Newport is compared with Aeneas as he sails up the James River in search of a safe landing place:

> At length, after much and wary search (with their barge coasting still before, as Vergil writeth Aeneas did, arriving in the region of Italy called Latium upon the banks of the River

Tiber)…they had sight of an extended plain. (Strachey, *A Voyage to Virginia*, 1609, 78)

Later as Strachey describes the landfall as a low plain of about half an acre, he adds, "or so much as Queen Dido might buy of King Iarbas, which she compassed with the thongs cut out of one bull hide and therein built her castle of Byrsa." Howard Mumford Jones has suggested that the *Aeneid* also informs the organization of *The Proceedings of the English Colonie in Virginia*, published at Oxford in 1612. The *Proceedings*, written in twelve books (as was the *Aeneid*), makes of Captain John Smith an Aeneas figure, while Powhatan becomes strangely like Turnus (Jones, *O Strange New World*, 1964, 238).

The story of the *Aeneid* parallels the imagery it provided for America: a westward journey filled with perils and false starts, transporting a people under divine guidance to new shores in a new land. While George Washington was not classically educated and his choice in art no doubt reflected the prevailing taste of his time, it seems significant that upon his retirement from the military service he ordered for Mount Vernon a sculpture of Aeneas carrying his father out of Troy.

Whereas the American South was something of a "New Rome," the Puritans in New England created what we might call a "New Jerusalem." Louis P. Simpson neatly describes the identification of New England with the Ancient Israelites:

> The new rise of New England as a spiritual nation was integral to the origins of New England, which was established as the result of an exodus of a chosen people from an old England, a world in which they had become spiritual aliens. To purify and to fulfill their personal and corporate relationship to God, they set out on an "errand into the wilderness," explicitly identifying their errand with that of the Israelites. (Simpson, *The Man of Letters in New England and the South*, 1973, 203)

Colonial New England was a theocracy dominated by a powerful and highly educated clergy. It was not easy for those clerics to reconcile their spiritual mission with their legacy of "pagan" literature. In 1726 Cotton Mather denounced Homer's treatment of the gods as opening "the Floodgates for a prodigious Inundation of wickedness to break in upon the nations," calling Homer "one of the greatest Apostles, the Devil ever had in the world" (*Manductio ad Ministerium*, 1726, 42). Elsewhere he warned against "a Conversation with the Muses that are no better than Harlots." And in a tribute to Ezekiel Cheever, his teacher, Mather praised the master for turning his students from Dido to David:

Young Au(gu)stin(e) wept, when he saw Dido dead,
Tho not a Tear for a Lost soul he had:
Our Master would not let us be so vain
But us from Virgil did to David train.
(Mather, *Corderius Americanus*, 1708, 31)

Nevertheless, Mather's great work *Magnalia Christi Americana*, completed in 1700, begins on a note of epic grandeur and intention: "I write the wonders of the Christian religion, flying from the Depravation of Europe to the American Strand." Leo M. Kaiser has identified thirty-one verse passages in the *Magnalia* that come from Vergil. Some are direct quotations, some adapted in various degrees of recognizability. All books of the *Aeneid* except 5, 8, 9, and 10 are represented. Thus Vergil also had a home in the New Jerusalem of New England, even if precariously perched in the "City set on a Hill."

Among American presidents, two of the best Vergilians, John Adams and Thomas Jefferson, died on the same day, July 4, 1826, exactly fifty years after the signing of the Declaration they had been chosen to draft. In 1756, the year following his graduation from Harvard, Adams set for himself the discipline of reading thirty or forty lines of Vergil every day. He appreciated the *Georgics* as well as the *Aeneid*, which he called a "well-ordered

48

Garden" and found superior to *Paradise Lost*, and after a terrible storm at sea during a voyage to France in 1778 he noted in his diary: "Every School Boy can turn to more than one description of a storm in Vergil."

Thomas Jefferson owned numerous texts and translations of Vergil in his extensive library and quoted him six times (four citations are from the *Aeneid*, two from the *Eclogues*) in his commonplace books. Jefferson's interest in poetry declined with age, however, so that at one point under the press of public responsibilities he wrote, "At present I cannot read even Vergil with pleasure."

John Adams's careful supervision of the classical studies of his son John Quincy Adams assured a place for Vergil in the imagination also of the sixth president of the United States. When the younger Adams was studying abroad in 1780–81, his father urged him to "study in Latin, above all, Vergil and Cicero." Between July 1783 and February 1784, John Quincy copied the entire Latin texts of the *Eclogues* and *Georgics*, providing a translation of the former in rhymed couplets and of the latter in prose. Among the six bronze busts in his study in Quincy, Massachusetts, his "household gods" as he called them, one was of Vergil.

Five years after the deaths of John Adams and Thomas Jefferson in 1826, the only man to become both a professional classicist and a president of the United States was born in a log cabin in Cuyahoga County, Ohio. James Abram Garfield was educated first at the nearby Geauga Academy, then at what became Hiram College, and finally was graduated from Williams College in 1856. After his graduation he returned to Hiram as a professor of ancient languages and literature. Shortly thereafter, at the age of twenty-six, he was chosen president of the college. Garfield's great love of the classics and his many intellectual interests—he was also the only U.S. president to devise a proof of the Pythagorean theorem—are fully documented in his extensive diaries.

The first mention of Vergil in the diaries appears on Wednesday, November 5, 1851, when Garfield was a student at the Eclectic Institute, later Hiram College: "I read 125 lines in Caesar today and finished the third book. I have undertaken to finish the fourth book this term which is as far as they generally read that Book. I shall then be ready for Vergil." By April 28, 1852, he was reading 30 lines of Vergil a day, 120 lines of Sallust, and 30 in Greek, in addition to classes in geometry and Greek and Latin grammar. The next night he wrote:

> I will spend a few moments after the labor of the evening has closed, in communing with my old friend, my journal. Well Sir! I have had good lessons today all throughout, and have done a good share towards those for tomorrow. . . . I enjoy very much the poetry of Vergil. We read today of a storm raised by Eolus the God of the winds who kept them chained in a hollow mountain, and for the sake of obtaining a nymph for a wife, he struck the side of the mountain, and the winds rush forth, mingling earth and heaven. His imagery is very beautiful, and truly belongs to an age of epics and lyrics.

By April of 1853 Garfield was teaching the Vergil class, assigning some seventy lines per lesson. Altogether he read some eight books of the *Aeneid* before transferring to Williams for his last two years of college.

Garfield had a highly disciplined mind, but it was the mind of a poet, not a pedant. He often wrote verse in his journals, and Horace was a special favorite. He loved words, and on September 28, 1857, he noted in his journal, "It is my chief joy in teaching the classes to study the wonders of words and their changes. I believe the history and philosophy and wonders of language is yet to be written if to be written at all."

Garfield's literary interests persisted as he moved into a political career, and he sometimes entertained his friends by writing Greek with one hand and Latin with the other—at the same time. When Congress was not in session he would often read and write about Horace. In 1872 he relates a conversation with a political friend, one Mr. Fish, on the subject of the national motto: "Mr. Fish told me he had been trying to trace the origin of our national motto, 'E Pluribus Unum' but could find no earlier trace than the Gentleman's Magazine established in 1754, on the tile page of which was a hand grasping a bunch of flowers, and under it the motto." Four years later, however, the problem was solved. On January 31, 1876, Garfield describes a visit to a friend's library: "Spent some time in the morning looking over Mr. Hoar's library. Among other things, he showed me a passage in line 102 of Vergil's 'Moretum,' in which occur these words: *color est e pluribus unus,* probably the origin of our national motto. The republic is a salad where many qualities and colors are united in one."

Garfield's short-lived term as president began and ended in 1881, the year that Europeans were observing the nineteen-hundredth anniversary of Vergil's death and that Tennyson was writing his remarkable tribute to "Roman Vergil." The silence about Vergil in the United States, however, was all but complete. As Meyer Reinhold writes: "By the last decades of the nineteenth century classical learning had ceased to provide moral, political, aesthetic models for educated Americans; it become the province of classical scholars." Even in the *Proceedings of the American Philological Association* for 1881, 1882, and 1883, Vergil is not mentioned at all.

The twentieth century saw a revival of the importance of Vergil to public life in America, at least in literature and, on one occasion, as part of the most august state occasion of all. The literary figure most sensitive to the applicability of the *Aeneid* to

51

contemporary America was the poet and critic Allen Tate. In three major poems in which Aeneas serves as narrator and in his only novel *The Fathers*, all written in the early 1930s after he had reread the *Aeneid* as an adult, Tate explores the ways in which Vergil's epic provides both a sense of continuity with the past and a measure by which to judge the fragmentation and decline of our culture. In "Aeneas at Washington" (1933) we see Aeneas at the outset of the poem reflecting on his past before assessing his present circumstance:

I saw myself saw furious with blood
Neoptolemus, at his side the black Atridae,
Hecuba and the hundred daughters, Priam
Cut down, his filth drenching the holy fires.
In that extremity I bore me well,
A true gentleman, valorous in arms.
Disinterested and honourable. Then fled:
That was a time when civilization
Run by the few fell to the many, and
Crashed to the shout of men, the clang of arms:
Cold victualing I seized, I hoisted up
The old man my father upon my back,
In the smoke made by sea for a new world
Saving little—a mind imperishable
If time is, a love of past things tenuous
As the hesitation of receding love.

* * *

I stood in the rain, far from home at nightfall
By the Potomac, the great Dome lit the water,
The city my blood had built I knew no more
While the screech owl whistled his new delight
Consecutively dark.

52

Stuck in the wet mire
Four thousand leagues from the ninth buried city
I thought of Troy, what we had built her for.
(Allen Tate, *The Swimmers and Other Selected Poems,* 1970, 5, 6)

Tate understood how little can be saved from the past and that what we save is tenuous. If time is imperishable, however, the legacy we carry is also imperishable. Here, that legacy has been sufficient to enable the founding of a new Rome on the banks of the Potomac. Its destiny, however, is by no means assured.

For the presidential inauguration of January 20, 1961, Robert Frost wrote "Dedication." Here Frost expresses an unalloyed national enthusiasm not characteristic even of Vergil:

Summoning artists to participate
In the august occasions of the state
Seems something artists ought to celebrate.
Today is for my cause a day of days.
And his be poetry's old-fashioned praise
Who was the first to think of such a thing.

Frost then provides "some preliminary history in rhyme," again with a Vergilian flavor:

"New order of the ages" did we say?
If it looks none too orderly today,
'Tis a confusion it was ours to start
So in it have to take courageous part.

The poem concludes with a celebratory connection with Vergil's own Augustan age:

It makes the prophet in us all presage
The glory of a next Augustan age
Of a power leading from its strength and pride
Of young ambition eager to be tried,
Firm in our free beliefs without 'dismay,
In any game the nations want to play.

A golden age of poetry and power
Of which this noonday's the beginning hour.
(Frost, *In the Clearing*, 1962, 28–30)

That Tate and Frost can find Vergil adaptable to two such different views of our condition demonstrates why Vergil has had a claim on the American imagination from the beginning of the European immigration. Vergil's applicability to our experience derives from four characteristics of his poetry. First, it is itself derivative, adapting the earlier Greek experience to that of Rome. Second, it is historical; Vergil is writing acutely aware of the historical situation he inhabits, not in a world of timeless abstractions. Next, it is political poetry; Vergil's concern with the politics of power of Rome is not foreign to the politics of the power of the United States. Finally, it is matchless poetry.

Vergil provides for us images, similes, and symbols by which to enlarge and explicate our cultural experience. Because we have Vergil, we are far less alone in the world and in time than otherwise we might be.

Connection

On Authoring and Authority
Why I Write

The words "authoring" and "authority" come from the same Latin verb, *augere*, meaning to enlarge or extend. That derivation is helpful in thinking about the relationship between writing and authority, specifically *narrative authority*, our standing within a story and the role of our writing in enlarging that narrative.

I once calculated how many generations of writers and teachers have passed down to me the *Aeneid* all the way from Vergil. I estimated the number to be sixty-seven, with my students now forming the sixty-eighth. When I write about Vergil I do so in the company of all those predecessors and even the successors to come. Their work informs mine, as mine will inform theirs.

With this continuity, humane studies form a whole cloth. By reading and teaching and writing about the texts we have inherited, we confirm and extend them. When the tradition is imperiled—and it always is—we engage in strategies to re-suture some of the tears in the fabric.

In other ways, what we write can and ought to be discontinuous, perhaps radically discontinuous, with the canon. The verb *augere* also means to increase in number, to make louder, or to intensify in emphasis or urgency. Sometimes our work is to offer not sutures but new structures. Here we help provide what Lucretius calls the *clinamen* or swerve by which change occurs in the universe.

Everyone who teaches does this already because each of us brings a different set of ideas to our texts. Then we begin asking the hard questions of who has established the prevailing interpretations and by what authority? Who is included, who has been left out, and why? Then we remember again that how things really are can never be singly and finally established. As one scholar puts it: "There are no 'brute facts'; there is only the mysterious, many-layered, always questionable total complex of . . . historical experience" (Heinrich Ott, *Interpretation: The Poetry of Meaning*, 1967, 32–33.) It is this doubleness that reserves a place for mystery in the life of the mind.

The task of revising the tradition belongs not just to the humanities. All of our disciplines tend to make of themselves cults in which only the initiated few are communicants. The gates to the temples open only to the passwords of our jargon and turn only on the hinges of our methodologies.

Sociologist Richard H. Brown urges an aesthetic for his discipline that is metaphorical and ironic—and thus more revelatory of human experience than statistics:

> In this sense social theories can be on the side either of piety or of profanation, in favor of order or of renovation. They can sanctify the conventional by formalizing it in occult language or they can demystify the sacrosanct by formally exposing its contradictions. . . . In opening the sacred to scrutiny, sociology at once profanes and purifies it. Sociology's truth is truth in the original Greek sense: "the unconcealing of what is concealed." (Brown, *A Poetic for Sociology*, 1977, 232–33)

So it is that when we write, we assume our authority for both the continuation *and* the revision of the canon. Two other consequences of writing, however, relate not to the tradition but to ourselves.

First, writing augments and enlarges us. Writing is productive. When we write, things happen that we did not expect in advance. "How do I know what I think until I see what I say?"

asks E. M. Forster. Those who have studied the cognitive process of writing suggest that the act of writing itself serves as a means by which we discover what it is we have to say.

How we understand cognition bears significantly on how we understand issues of certainty and therefore issues of authority. The creative part of the human brain does not receive messages directly. Rather, out of all the available evidence it forms theories of what the world is like, then matches new evidence to the theories. In his *Unification of Fundamental Forces* (1990), Nobel Laureate Abdus Salam quotes Einstein as having said to Heisenberg: "Whether you can observe a thing or not depends on the theory which you use. It is the theory which decides what can be observed."

By writing we therefore extend ourselves. But in writing we also change ourselves. Writing is a severe and humbling taskmaster. Once we have written on a subject, our writing has changed us as much as we have broken down and reshaped the material itself. And once that has happened, we assume the best kind of authority, the kind that is intrinsic to our texts, our disciplines, and our own experience of the world.

These are some of the consequences and conditions of our writing, but the question remains: Why write at all? I can think of five reasons.

First, we write because we can. For those whom society has afforded the training, the resources, and even the time to write, one might even say we have an obligation to write.

Second, we write out of gratitude. We write an article or an essay or a book because of all the articles, essays, and books we have read. Our writing is a recognition of all those who have brought us this far. It is a return on their investment.

Third, we write as an act of hospitality to strangers. In an earlier period of my life I thought of writing as the most private of acts, the work of seclusion far from the claims of the public realm. Now I see writing as the most public thing we can do because it touches people we will never meet, some of whom will come after us. Writing is meeting. We are hosts, inviting a company of strangers to gather around the words we offer in hospitality.

Fourth, we write to persuade, because we care about something passionately, because we are committed enough to grind ourselves up and do it again and again until we get it right, as right as we can get it. The very best writing in our disciplines does not cover up this passion. The very worst writing in our professions does, pretending a false authority of objectivity. The Nobel prize-winning scientist Isador Isaac Rabi urges: "Take your profession personally."

Finally—and I know no way to say this except directly—we write for the joy of it. The joy when the idea first comes and then when the argument or poem or story comes together at the end more than compensates for the anxiety of the waiting and the burden of the work.

There are meanings to be found, symbolic codes to be maintained, received traditions to be revised. Our writing creates the condition of those possibilities. We live in an untidy and uncertain world, but with the authority of those twenty-six cunning conjurors of the alphabet, we can mobilize our stories in the face of it.

Hospitality
Welcoming Strangers

One day I drove from the farm to a small town nearby to locate a welder to help with some minor repairs. When I phoned the gentlemen whom someone in the town recommended, his wife told me that he was out but would be home soon. I stopped by later, knocking tentatively at the back door because it was lunch time. His wife answered and invited me to come in and join them for lunch.

I was in the process of declining, saying I would come back later, when the welder himself appeared, napkin in hand. He also urged me to come in for lunch and added a description of the food on the table. My real hunger overcame my theoretical inhibitions, and I accepted. Many stories were shared and plates passed before my hosts asked my name, my purpose for coming, or the most important question in that culture, who my people were.

What I was offered that day was an act of hospitality in the ancient sense, not the modern. Modern hospitality is a transaction among friends, for example an invitation to close acquaintances to come for dinner or a party. Ancient hospitality is a transaction among strangers. In antiquity the relationship between host and stranger was so charged and precarious that the gods—Zeus Xenios in the Greek world and Yahweh in the Hebrew—take care to protect it. The Talmud boldly asserts that hospitality to strangers is greater than welcoming the presence of God.

Even people we know best—spouses, children, friends— all are strangers. I knew my cherished brother for thirty-four years before I knew he was gay. And if we have them, our children are strangers, too. There are things about them we will never know. It was a stranger, not a beloved four-year old son, who said to me one day, "There aren't any grown-ups. There are only grown-bigs. God is the only grown-up." Our parents, whether they are living are not, are also strangers to us. We are able to know them even less well than our children, and we will keep discovering things about them long after they are dead.

Differences always distinguish us in this patchwork world. One way of honoring difference is to welcome strangers with an act of hospitality that does not stem from familiarity or affection or approval. The ancients believed that the stranger at our door might even be a divinity.

The stranger is also our self. We have all experienced the feeling that we are somehow excluded from the "magic circle" of those who are truly accepted. In *Outside the Magic Circle*, Virginia Foster Durr describes growing up as a belle and debutante in Birmingham, Alabama. She made the mistake of going to college in the North and getting strange ideas about race. She made the mistake also of being the sister-in-law of U.S. Supreme Court Justice Hugo Black, vilified in the South for his support of racial integration. After serving with her husband in the New Deal and suffering later as a victim of the McCarthy era, Virginia Durr moved back to Alabama, still outside the magic circle but surrounded by admirers near and far.

My own sense of outsideness started early and stayed late: as a girl among brothers; as a liberal at the University of Texas; as a Southerner in New York; as a white faculty member at Fisk University; as a female faculty member at Vanderbilt University; as a Latin teacher in the modern world; and, sometimes I presume to think, as a Christian in the Bible Belt.

Gradually, however, I came to feel at home outside the magic circle. As we move from the need for approval from others to a feeling of being situated within ourselves—that is, as we move from heteronomy to autonomy—we become more and more of a stranger to ourselves. When we are seeking approval from other people, we know exactly what we think they want us to be. That is easy and familiar. When we move toward autonomy, however, we are less sure of ourselves as we seek to discern the unique thing that only we can do, the particular person that only we can be.

In the Jewish and Christian traditions, God is a stranger, too, the strangest of all. One time when Jesus was praying alone, his disciples appeared and he asked them, "Who do the people say that I am?" They answered that some said John the Baptist and others said Elijah and still others said a prophet of old who had risen again. Then Jesus pressed them, "But who do you say that I am?" Peter responded, "The Christ of God." At that point Jesus enjoined them not to tell this to anybody. He explained that he was going to suffer and be rejected, and therefore they were not to tell anyone.

In one sense, this story argues for the greatest reticence in mentioning the name of God. This is part and parcel of the courtesy of orthodox Jews who refuse to write the name of God, a presumption that God can be defined by human beings. It is the courtesy of Dietrich Bonhoeffer in a Nazi prison who said that he was more comfortable naming God to non-believers than to believers. And it is the courtesy that informs Phillip Roth's short story, "The Conversion of the Jews."

In that story thirteen-year-old Oscar Friedman is preparing for his bar-mitzvah with Rabbi Bender. Oscar has the unfortunate habit of asking unexpected questions. When he gets conventional answers, he says to the rabbi: "But I meant something different." The rabbi is not amused, and when this happens once too often, he calls Oscar's mother, advising her to ask her son what the problem was at the bar-mitzvah class. Oscar tells her:

I asked the question about God, how, if He could create the heaven and earth in six days and make all the animals and the fish and the light in six days—the light especially, that's what always gets me—that He can make the light. Anyway, I asked Rabbi Bender if He could make all that in six days, and if God could pick the six days he wanted right out of nowhere, why couldn't he let a woman have a baby without having intercourse.

Oscar's mother slapped him when she heard the question, just as Rabbi Bender had done. The conflict escalates until finally Oscar runs to the top of the synagogue and threatens to jump. A crowd gathers below on the street, begging him not to. Finally Oscar shouts down to his mother and the Rabbi: "Promise me, promise me you'll never hit anybody about God. You should never hit anybody about God."

Oscar Friedman was worried not so much about the virgin birth as about our hitting people in the name of God. He knew that when we hit people because of what we think we know about God, we do not know God.

Oscar was arguing for a conversion to courtesy toward the stranger who is God and toward all the strangers who are God's people.

He was arguing for hospitality.

Recalling Melanoia
When I didn't know myself

Even now I shrink from telling how it was for me those deathly months.

Depression is the common name for what I experienced, but I have devised a more descriptive term: "Melanoia." It means "obsessed with darkness." For three seasons, I was afflicted.

Through the fall semester at my university I was able to meet my teaching and other obligations, but just barely. As December fell, everything became worse. By late February I could not return to the classroom after spring break. For four weeks I missed teaching my classes altogether. My colleagues filled in for me, with no words of complaint I ever heard. Around early April I began to surface again toward the sun.

I will not recount how I got into this melanoia, how eventually I came, and was helped, through it, or what I learned from it. Those stories are particular to me and are of no general interest. I seek instead to describe as accurately as I can, from the inside, the darkness of the worst time. The idea of this telling first came to me while writing a note to a friend whose daughter committed suicide. "If anyone should be so tactless," I wrote, "as to ask you how could she have *done* that, please refer that person to me. I know. It's practically all I thought about for months."

But *why?* I ask myself. *Why?* Why revisit hell?

Perhaps I make this accounting to provide company for some other soul, known or unknown to me, mired in the same depths. I did *not* say I do it to help someone else. When I was in the lightless place, I sought no advice, did not welcome it, did not believe it when it came. Hell is inimical to advice.

Maybe I write because to leave it out would be a lie about my life.

Maybe I write from simple gratitude that I am here to tell this story.

Maybe I tell it out of the curiosity behind a promise I made to myself long ago:

Positive

Think positive, chirped the worker
at the gym as I left for the good day
I was instructed also to have.

How, I thought, in her innocence
could she presume to fit the same advice
to every stranger she salutes?

At the moment I passed her by
I was plumbing the murk, dead set
on making sense of some unopinioned dark.

For an instant I was enticed to hoist
my sail wide and white as a smile,
set to scud breezily into the day.

But, being peculiarly curious,
I held instead to the work of discerning
what is below the surface I traverse

so when I arrive at the other side
I'll know the whole of where I've been,

the reefs as well as the gleamy sea.

Profound depression is ineffable. The brooding silence overwhelms not because mental torment is more acute than physical pain, although depression is also physical, and not because of willful stubbornness on the part of the sufferer. Rather, it overwhelms because the same brain shredded by depression mutes its own powers of cognition. Depression turns one's brain to mush. Judgment is distorted. Aesthetic sensibility shuts down. All sensibility shuts down. During those long months I remember only one scrap of color, a yellow ribbon on a basket of fruit sent by a friend.

* * *

These things I remember:

I hated to hear the rising chatter of the birds early in the morning. That meant it was eighteen hours until I could go to sleep again.

I wanted to be in bed. All the time. I would do almost anything to get back to it. This was the closest I could come to oblivion.

All current events were bad. I could not bear to glance at a newspaper or be in the presence of a television or radio.

I was sure I was going to lose my job.

Emails piled up unanswered. I shuddered even knowing they were there.

I was paranoid about everything.

I hated the telephone. I cringed every time it rang, fearing I might have to speak to someone.

In the grocery store or out walking with A. anywhere in public, I hated to see people I knew. I was sure they would think ill of me for whatever reason.

* * *

As chair of my department, I answered to the dean. Sometime in the fall I went to see him, to inform him about my situation. I said, "I do not want to burden you, but for your information, due to depression, I am not functioning at a level I'm happy with in the department. And I know it shows. This needs to be on the table."

And, "Yes," I assured him when he asked, "I am getting good help."

R. replied: "No one has noticed. Take care of yourself. Keep working at your very low level of productivity and embarrassing everyone else. This is *only* by your high standards. I'm glad you trusted me to come."

Months later, in the worst time, he visited me at home. A dean who makes house calls!

I asked a psychiatrist what was wrong with suicide. I received two salutary answers: "It's a form of murder for one thing. For another, it's illegal." I had not considered either of those fundamental facts.

I learned that the psychiatrist and the family therapist I saw were courting danger all through those months. They knew what was preoccupying my dark mind, and if they did not act to assure my physical safety—usually by hospitalization—they could be held legally liable. I had to make promises to them repeatedly not to hurt myself.

At my request a lawyer friend sent me the specifics of the statutes:

Professionals are obligated to predict, warn or take protection if they know someone is talking about suicide (*TCA* 33-3-206).

An officer can arrest without a warrant anyone who is attempting to commit suicide (*TCA* 40-7-103 [5]).

Finally, a person is justified in threatening or using force, but not deadly force, against another when and to the degree the person reasonably believes the force is immediately necessary to prevent the other from committing suicide or from the self-infliction of serious bodily injury (*TCA* 39-11-613).

* * *

A. took me on long car trips, two up into Kentucky. I was mute and miserable. I did, however, find one pastime, one only, on which I could focus attention: I could make lists of words out of the letters of a word. Take, for example, *restaurant:* rest, test, nest, run, ran, tan, turn, sun, taunt, rant, sat, rat, stare, tear, rerun, runt, stunt, rate, tune, tent, ant, eat, treat, nature, set, use, rate, seer, ruse, rust, trust, tea, nut, stunt, state, sear, rear, art.

C.W. sent me a fruit basket and thoughtful counsel: "Volunteer. Schedule something every day with a friend. Write poetry. Cook good food. Do yoga. Read the Psalms. Change some things." This was all pre-mature at the time, but I remembered. When the time finally came that I could, I acted on his advice.

Notes from Friends

From L.K., after her luncheon in February I forced myself to attend:

So great to be with you yesterday—as it always is.

I don't know how to say this diplomatically, so I'll just jump in . . . . I don't know if it was my imagination or not, but I thought you seemed—preoccupied?? Not a good description, but that's the best I can come up with. Something weighing on your mind and heart, perhaps?

Forgive me, please, for treading where I have no right to go, but I love you so much, and just want to express my concerns (too strong)—no, my thoughts.

No answer required—none expected.

How brave and wonderful of L. to risk writing that. Thank you, dear friend.

From C.B.:

This card makes me recall the many happy times we have had together with a cup of tea or coffee. We will enjoy these times again. You are loved by all we know and especially by G. and me.

From a student:

Dear Professor Wiltshire,

It was so good to see you in the Vergil seminar today. . . . If there's anything I can do for you, please let me know. I'm serious—laundry, cleaning house, anything—you shouldn't be doing it, and I don't mind at all. I'm going to be in Nashville for the summer, too, so please don't hesitate to ask a favor.

The most important thing is your getting better! The rest will work itself out. Take care of yourself. I hope to see you soon.

From J.B. "A Get-Well Wish for my Friend"

Dearest Susan,

Come anytime you want to. I think God is trying to tell you to be not afraid of the circumstances in which you find yourself. God simply promises not to abandon us but to go with us through the darkness of fear or uncertainty.

My daughter said: "Don't go anywhere, Mommie. I need you to show me how to be pregnant and how to pick out china." My son, when terrified I asked him "What if this happens to me again?" said, simply, "Then we will take care of you again."

My older brother Davis wrote:

Susan, Thanks so much for the card and quotes. You are an amazing person. How did God shower me with such a mother and sister? More than I deserve!" [I had never heard such words from him before.]

I realized in retrospect I had a minyan, a holy group of ten who would not let me go.

An Argument
(found in a scrap of notes)

Depression	Me
I'll tire you out	But I'm tough—and I've defeated you before
You're toast	Or maybe, as I told my friend forty years ago, "I'll do my best work in my 60's!"
No one respects you anymore	If that's so, too bad.
You are not only not "perfect," you're lousy.	I'm human, which is more than you can say for yourself.
I about got you this time	No, you didn't even come close.
You don't have any more causes. You're history.	Could be—but I doubt it.
You're a sorry teacher	I need to work harder on my teaching. But I'm not bad either.
I've got you feeling sorry for yourself	Let me tell you again: I'm another struggling member of the human race.
[Silence]	And besides, that status

came from the grace of
God, Buster, not from you
Not
Who appointed you God?
Only God is God. You are
a distortion and a fraud.
You're evil. Get behind me.

Life is a drag though
I want you to check out

I'm in your mind.
You're stuck with me.
And even if I don't
get you this time,
I'll be back

Wrong customer.

You won't get me this time.
And if you come back, you
won't get me then either,
ever. You are mean as sin
and low as dirt.

Ah yes, but I've got
the chemical upper hand
in your brain

You think so, but I have an
arsenal far vaster than
yours on my side
(including, but not limited
to, pharmaceuticals).

OK—but you're never going
to write another book.

Maybe not. But you don't
know that and neither do I.

You've never written anything
any good anyway.
Life is no good.

Wrong.
Life is a gift I never even
asked for.

* * *

C.B. came. I went with her to get a haircut. Agony to be in a beauty salon or anywhere else. Today it seems again as if all is in confusion, except the love and support of dear ones closest by.

What would I think of someone else in my state? I hope I would have more compassion than blame.

My affairs and files in such disarray. It would be unethical to leave such a mess.

I am sick and tired of being sick and tired. Tired of being so negative about almost everything. Tired of not exercising. Too tired to exercise. I gnaw on these worries:

- Being like this for the rest of my life
- Letting my family down
- The house being robbed
- Losing the farm and cattle
- That I have become or will become a recluse
- That I have lapsed into total narcissism
- That I'm losing my mind and personal pride
- I used to be the "take a chance" person in our family. Why or how did that change?
- I feel judged by everything now
- The most awful tedium is the self-absorption – a quality I decry in others
- I worry about impulsiveness and sheer stupidity.

* * *

J.E. pushed me hard this morning, trying to force me out from under the rock lying on top of me: "I've recently been to several funerals. I don't want to go to another one." He got my attention.

Perhaps such a long dark season can produce clearing places for new crops and more space for time with kites and kin.

* * *

71

Mere surviving is paltry, the other side of selfish. But even thriving can be selfish if not in community and service. To thrive is to be in daily life.

* * *

And finally—

April 5: As of tonight, I hope to go to school tomorrow afternoon, for a gentle pass-through.

April 6: Went to school for an hour and a half today. It felt very good.

Lux lucit in tenebris

Light shines in darkness

Lucile's Last Days

One Friday morning at the age of ninety-six, Lucile Davis Ford fell and broke her hip. She was in terrible pain. When the paramedics arrived and told her they had to pick her up, she said, "O.K. And by the way, do you know the derivation of the term O.K.?" She explained that it became a slogan during the presidential election of 1840 for Martin Van Buren, known as "Old Kinderhook," from his birthplace in New York State.

For two days in the hospital Lucile and the family considered the consequences of her undergoing surgery for a hip replacement. Then, on Sunday, January 9, I awoke in the hospital room at 4:30 AM to hear Lucile saying firmly: "This is the last day of my life. I have made my decision. I don't want help for anything. I just want to go back to my pretty home and die. Aesthetics are important to me."

She insisted I call my brother Davis, right then, with this information. I said I would dial, but Lucile had to do the talking. Lucile repeated the same determined decision to Davis, who arrived at the hospital shortly thereafter. With the cooperation of the doctors and the agreement of the family (it would not have deterred Lucile if we had disagreed), she moved on Sunday to Christopher House, the Hospice Austin residential facility.

After she made her decision, Lucile said, "It makes me feel good to be in charge of my death. Most people can't be in charge of their death, but I can. I'm blessed. It's a gift to me. This was nobody's idea but my own. If I felt vigorous, I could take anything. But I don't. I'm tired of it. I want to control my own ease. You can't imagine how relieved I feel to have it settled. I didn't feel relieved when I fell, but I do now. There's no future at all for me physically. I can't wait to get out of this physical shell I'm in."

The doctor knocked on the door. My daughter, Carrie, asked Lucile if she wanted her lipstick. "Well, of course!" she answered.

When someone asked her if she wanted some water, she said, "I'd rather have sherry."

"I came in beloved. I go out beloved. What more can you ask?"

The ambulance ride to the hospice was excruciatingly painful for Lucile. As the paramedics were loading her, she said, "I haven't died before, so I haven't learned the technique." Since there was nothing else to do, I said, "Mom, I know this won't help you, but it will help me, so I am going to quote your favorite poem to make this ride go faster." I began Rupert Brooke's "The Soldier": "If I should die, think only this of me: / That there's some corner of a foreign field / That is forever England . . ." When she got to the last lines, I forgot a phrase. Lucile supplied it, and we finished the poem in unison: "And laughter, learnt of friends; and gentleness / In hearts at peace, under an English heaven."

When Lucile woke up in Christopher House on Monday, January 10, she said, "This hasn't happened before in the history of the world." I assured her it had not, since no one like her had existed before in the history of the world. Lucile drifted off to sleep. When she woke up, she said, "*Requiescat in pace.*" I laughed: "Mother, you are the only person in the world who could wake up on her deathbed quoting Latin!"

Not long after, Davis walked in. "This is the last round-up," she announced to him. How could she come up with exactly the right greetings for her Latin teacher daughter and her cowboy son?

"It's been a noble going away," she said to us both. "Your

presence. I'd call this a pretty nice going home. You two are so cute."

Her granddaughter Kristy assured her, "It's going to be so beautiful." Lucile responded firmly, "It's already been beautiful here, so I have no worries."

Carrie asked her, "Are you scared, Boo?" "No," she said, "I'm just bored. Let's call a spade a spade."

She followed with a whole series of observations that were pure Lucile:

I want to go out on a high note. My life has been nothing but love. I appreciate that more than I can say.

I don't look for trouble. Much.

I'm not raising Cain. Just Abel.

I said, "I love you, Mom." Lucile returned: "We've already established that. Let's not go through it again. We don't need rehearsals."

Later she added: "We are all God's children." (Pause) "I'm trying to think of something noble to say."

When Davis left, Lucile said, "He's run out of cute things to say, so he's leaving." Davis always was the one to make us laugh.

On Monday evening, the family went out for Mexican food. Many margaritas helped celebrate Lucile's life. Our children, Matthew and Carrie, stayed behind with their grandmother. Matt took notes.

"Not everybody gets a send-off like this," Lucile said to them.

Matthew asked her what she loved most about travel. "Learning," she answered.

When the subject of Australia came up, Lucile spoke at length of our father's helping introduce the Murray Grey cattle breed from Australia to America. She said: "Frank loved breeding cattle and was good at it. He loved the Murray Greys; they adapted well to this country. He would order sperm and artificially breed them. It's really a very interesting process. Frank would love to know that you are thinking about a new breed as I am passing on. I wasn't disinterested in raising cattle. It's just that my main interest was in raising a family. I enjoyed being a good mother. I think I was."

At one point Carrie helped put her raised arms down, crossed below her chest. Boo laughed and said, "I don't mean to look pious."

"Enjoy every day because they're important."

On Tuesday morning, January 11, Lucile woke up early. "I woke up," she said. "I thought I had died. But I woke up. Darn it." At one point leaving the room, Davis said, "Lucile, don't go anywhere until I get back." She smiled in complicity.

That evening Lucile went to sleep and died shortly after midnight.

Equality

Carrie Chapman Catt and the Vote for Women
How one person changed the world

In a schoolyard in Iowa in 1870, Carrie Chapman Catt's brother picked up a garter snake and proceeded to terrorize all the girls on the playground. Eleven-year old Carrie ran away from the schoolyard with the other girls, but as she ran she was thinking: *The snake must be harmless, or else my brother would not have picked it up.* Further, she knew how much fun he was having scaring all the girls. The next morning, Carrie found a similar snake and went after her brother with the creature in her hand and purpose in her eye. That put an end to his bullying. It was a lesson Carrie Chapman Catt never forgot. If the cause is right and the bullies know you mean business, the rules change.

Carrie attended college at what is now Iowa State University in Ames. Among her many other activities she was a member of the Crescent Literary Society, which did not allow women to speak in meetings. Carrie spoke anyway. Long debate about the issue followed. The ban was lifted. Carrie graduated in 1880 as valedictorian of her class and became a law clerk, a teacher, and then superintendent of schools in Mason City, Iowa.

After her first husband died within a year of their marriage, she moved to San Francisco and in 1890 married George Catt, a prosperous engineer whom she had known in college. George Catt was also an ardent advocate for women's rights and all his life supported Carrie both financially and personally in her work for women's suffrage. That same year at the age of twenty-seven, the brilliant young activist attended her first national suffrage convention.

Catt's hardest campaign was her first when she went to South Dakota to help organize the fledgling movement there for a state suffrage amendment. She traveled alone from train stop to train stop, often spending the night in the tiny, crowded houses of farm families. On one occasion she got off the train at an empty grain elevator without a soul in sight. Much later, an elderly man came to get her in a wagon to take her to his home. A five-year drought had ravaged the state, and they could offer her nothing to eat but bread and watermelons.

That evening inside the grain elevator before a gathering of some forty farm families, their babies on blankets on the floor, Carrie spoke *about the need for women's suffrage.* Catt knew that political corruption had been widespread and that the anti-suffrage forces had bought the required votes in advance. She wrote at the time: "Ours is a cold, lonesome little movement which will make our hearts ache about November 5. We need some kind of political mustard plaster to make things lively. We are appealing to justice for success, when it is selfishness that governs mankind." When election day came, 45,000 votes were cast against the amendment, 22,000 in favor. The South Dakota campaign, however, accomplished one crucial result. It taught Carrie Chapman Catt what was essential for winning at the polls: endorsements by large citizens' organizations, endorsements by the major political parties, money, and organization. Never again would she go into a campaign with all the cards stacked against her.

The proposed amendment granting women the right to vote had been first introduced into Congress in 1878. It reads: "The right of citizens of the United States to vote shall not be denied or abridged by the United States or by any State on account of sex."

For over forty years Congress refused to pass the amendment. Finally, the House and Senate narrowly approved the measure in 1919 and submitted it to the states for ratification. In fairly short order, thirty-five states ratified the amendment, but one more state was needed before women's suffrage would become the law of the land. Tennessee was considered the most likely possibility. The time allotted for passage was running out, and so was the administration of President Woodrow Wilson, who supported the measure. That is why Carrie Chapman Catt came to Nashville in the summer of 1920 for a weekend and stayed six weeks to direct the Tennessee campaign for passage.

The ground had been prepared for suffrage in Tennessee before Catt checked into at the Hermitage Hotel that hot summer day in 1920. Suffrage activities began in the state in 1876 with an address to a state political convention by Mrs. Napoleon Cromwell who urged a resolution in support of the vote for women. Her appeal seemed a preposterous joke to the delegates, and not until 1889 did the state's first equal suffrage society organize in Memphis.

Unsympathetic public opinion was so daunting that only an intrepid few would open their doors to suffrage meetings. The momentum grew, however, and in 1911 Mrs. Guilford Dudley was elected president of the newly formed Nashville Equal Suffrage League. The League sponsored a lecture at the Ryman auditorium by the militant Sylvia Pankhurst in 1912, and four years later the Vanderbilt suffrage league invited Sylvia's equally militant mother, Emmeline, to lecture.

The National American Women Suffrage Association held its national convention in Nashville in 1914. Mrs. Dudley considered this the turning point of the suffrage struggle in Tennessee, observing that the social side of the convention brought many society women into suffrage work.

But opposition was bitter. Religious leaders exhorted that God's punishment of women for Eve's apple-biting was to stay home ruled over by their husbands. John Vertrees, husband of the first president of the Tennessee anti-suffrage association, published his own statement of opposition, "An address to the Men of Tennessee on Female Suffrage," declaring that the problem was not a question of what women *wanted* but what they *ought to have.*

Governor A. H. Roberts convened a special session of the legislature on August 9, 1920. After a vote of twenty-five to four in the Senate in favor of suffrage, the House was tied at forty-eight to forty-eight until Harry T. Burn, a young Republican from east Tennessee, changed his mind at the urging of his mother. After a number of futile maneuvers by opponents, Roberts signed the certificate of ratification on August 24, and on August 26, 1920, the U.S. Secretary of State proclaimed the equal suffrage amendment to be part of the American Constitution.

After the Nineteenth Amendment was ratified in 1920, Catt wrote an account of the effort it required. What Catt did not point out in her list was the obvious fact that every vote in every campaign had to be cast by men. To get that word, *male,* out of the Constitution, she said, cost the women of this country

- fifty-two years of pauseless campaigns
- 56 state referendum campaigns
- 480 legislative campaigns to get state amendments submitted
- 47 state constitutional convention campaigns
- 277 state party convention campaigns
- 30 national party campaigns to get suffrage planks in the party platforms;
- 19 campaigns with 129 successive Congresses to get the federal amendment submitted

- and the final ratification campaign.

She continued:

> Millions of dollars were raised, mostly in small sums, and spent with economic care. Hundreds of women gave the accumulated possibilities of an entire lifetime; thousands gave years of their lives, hundreds of thousands gave constant interest and such aid as they could. It was a continuous and seemingly endless chain of activity. Young suffragists who helped form the last links of that chain were not born when it began. Old suffragists who helped forge the first links were dead when it ended.

Carrie Chapman Catt's leadership resulted from a combination of significant gifts: a forceful speaking style, personal dignity together with charm and humor, shrewd skills at political organization, and courage. She was at her best when the fight was fiercest, and she never gave up. She always couched the immediate issues in the larger background of their philosophical and social significance. For her, the vote was never an end but always the means to a more equitable, humane, and peaceful society.

Twenty YEARS LATER

In 1940, Eleanor Roosevelt wrote in *Good Housekeeping*:

> On the whole, during the last twenty years, government has been taking increasing cognizance of humanitarian questions, things that deal with the happiness of human beings, such as health, education, security. There is nothing, of course, to prove that this is entirely because of the women's interest, and yet I think it is significant that this change has come about during the period when women have been exercising their franchise.

Be Ye Therefore Whole
A Grammatical Problem

"Be ye therefore perfect, as your father in heaven is perfect" (Matt. 5.28). That passage in the Sermon on the Mount gave me a whole lot of trouble for the first half of my life. Children are literalists anyway, and as a pious Methodist girl given to seriousness, I was determined to achieve perfection. For me early on that meant not to smoke, drink, or consort with those who did. Later in young adulthood, it meant I personally had to do everything I thought needed to be done and to do it well. It about wore me out.

As the women's movement came along, I remarked to my friend Ed Bacon: "Ed, isn't it a shame that women who have a vocation and family as well as social and political commitments feel they have to be superwomen?" Ed responded, "No, the shame is that men are not expected to do all those things, too."

I finally realized that the problem with *perfect* is a grammatical problem. *Perfect* in Latin means thoroughly finished, completed action in past time. All over. It's no different in the original Greek of the Matthew text: The word *teleios* means the end of time, the end of things. Until the end time comes and I'm thoroughly finished—whenever and however that happens—I want to continue to grow and change. An amoeba is whole, but it shifts around. All living things do. I want to be whole—maybe even wholesome—but not over and done with.

Carl Jung says there are male and female elements in each one of us. He uses the terms *animus* for male and *anima* for female. If we make parallel lists of the qualities that are traditionally considered male or female, it might look something like this:

father/mother; provider/nurturer; thinker/feeler. The male might traditionally be thought to be more concerned about ends, about product, the female more about means, about process. We might also use the terms prophet and priest: the one coming from afar to judge and exhort, the other loving us and nurturing us through. Someone said that a prophet without a priest is as dangerous as a priest without a prophet. Male qualities without female qualities are as dangerous as female qualities without male qualities.

How do we put these two things together? Sociologist Alice Rossi has developed three models, three forms or possibilities for ordering relationships between majority and minority groups, between male and female, white and black, oppressor and oppressed. The first of these is the pluralist model, which affirms that each group has values and strengths of its own, that their complementarity defines them, and that everything works out all right as long as each group is doing what is appropriate to it. This would be, I think, the position of most anti-feminists. The problem with the pluralist model is that it never works, because if one group has power and the other does not, then the roles and worth of each group are always defined by the powerful group. The pluralist model makes it possible for men to be very creative or to put all their energies into their profession or whatever. But that freedom always requires a support group. Such an arrangement is functional for the dominant group, but it is not fully human for anybody.

Next is the assimilation model, which assumes that the minority group will gradually be absorbed into the mainstream by losing its distinguishing characteristics and acquiring the characteristics of the majority group. Some feminists, perhaps cynically, subscribe to this model. At least it rejects the idea of determinative psychological differences between male and female, but it also assumes that the world created by the majority group is the ideal, the best of all possible worlds.

The third model Rossi calls the hybrid model. It anticipates the society in which both the ascendant group and the minority group are capable of change. Indeed, it requires changes in both.

Some feminists have rejected the religious tradition, particularly the Christian tradition, because it has been used and is still being used to reinforce the submissive, inferior status of women. One such feminist is Mary Daly, who in a new preface to her book *The Church and the Second Sex* defines herself as a "post-Christian feminist" who can no longer subscribe to a tradition that has been used so effectively to subjugate women.

But the Bible nurtures its own seeds of criticism that lead to a very different conclusion. We read in Proverbs 31.10–12, often used in Mother's Day sermons, "A good wife who can find? She is far more precious than jewels. The heart of her husband trusts in her, and he will have no lack of gain. She does him good and not harm all the days of her life." That is wonderfully descriptive of a good, loving wife, a good Southern girl, a passive, dependent person.

Frequently, however, other verses in the same chapter are not quoted: "She is like the ships of the merchant. She brings her food from afar" (14). "She considers the field and buys it; with the fruit of her hands, she plants a vineyard" (16). "She girds her loins with strength and makes her arms strong" (17). "She makes linen garments and sells them; she delivers girdles to the merchant. Strength and dignity are her clothing, and she laughs at the time to come" (24–25). Here we get a very different picture of a strong, competent, capable human being. She is a farmer, a merchant, a manager, an entrepreneur.

Other biblical passages also transcend patriarchy. In Numbers 11:12, for example, God is a nursing mother: "Did I conceive all this people? Did I bring them forth that thou shouldst say to me, 'Carry them in your bosom as a nurse carries the sucking child, to the land which thou didst swear to give to their fathers?'" If God can work full-time and still be a nursing mother, so can we. Again, from Isaiah 49:15: "Can a woman forget her sucking child, that she should have no compassion on the son of her womb? Even these may forget, yet I will not forget you." Also from Isaiah 66:13: "As one who his mother comforts, so will I comfort you."

Later on, when Jesus is getting ready to enter Jerusalem for the last time, he looks at the city and wishes he were, of all things, a mother hen: "Oh Jerusalem, Jerusalem, the city that murders the prophets and stones the messengers sent to her? How often have I longed to gather your children, as a hen gathers her brood under her wings" (Luke 13:34).

Dietrich Bonhoeffer talks about the biblical term *anthropos teleios*, the whole, complete, perfect person. He says that this refers to the whole person, not just to the inner self, and that the heart in the biblical sense is not the inward life but the whole person in relation to God. Elsewhere, Julius Lester refers to the term "perfect" in the Sermon on the Mount: "Be ye therefore perfect as your Father in Heaven is perfect." Lester says that frightens us and asks why that is so:

Is that why we try to recruit God to lead the revolutionary vanguard and join the women's movement? Is that why we get all tangled up in eschatologies and apocalypses? Or is it because Jesus told us in the most simple, straightforward language ever used what it is we are to do with our lives? But that is hard, Jesus, we say. Be perfect? Hey man, lighten up. It is easier to be black, white, male, female, or a theologian. It is easier to be those things than it is to be perfect. But that is precisely what Jesus said, 'Be ye therefore perfect'—and he wouldn't have said it if it wasn't possible.

Translate "perfect" as "whole," and all things are possible.

A Letter to My Daughter about Women's Equity at Vanderbilt
A Meditation on Loss and Repair

Dear Carrie,

You asked me to tell you about WEAV and the Langland case. This all happened at Vanderbilt University over three decades ago. You were five years old when it began and eight when it ended. I have three distinct memories of your involvement, which I will recount in due course.

I will begin with the facts of the matter, then tell you the lessons we learned in pursuing it. In 1975 the English department at Vanderbilt hired Elizabeth Langland as an assistant professor. One of her colleagues said at the time, "She was one of the two brightest new Ph.D.'s in English in the country, and we got her." Shortly after she arrived, Elizabeth was also appointed to head the Women's Studies Committee. We still had no program or full-time director. Among Elizabeth's research interests was the study of women in literature, and she was already publishing pioneering material in the field.

In time Elizabeth was recommended by her department for promotion with tenure, the first woman ever to be recommended for tenure in the hundred-year history of the English department. The vote was fifteen to five. We knew the identities of four of the five opponents—the same ones who resigned from the Episcopal Church when it started ordaining women. We were delighted by the other fifteen votes and the positive decision, though not surprised. Elizabeth was and is that good.

Several months later and after delaying word of his decision long after the usual announcement time in the spring, the dean of the college called the head of the English department on a Saturday morning in June—just before he left on vacation and when the campus was deserted—to say he did not concur with the department's decision and that it would not go forward. Elizabeth would have to leave Vanderbilt after one more year.

Elizabeth called when she heard. I asked her what she was going to do about it.

"I'm going to fight it," she said.

"Why?" I asked.

"So my daughter won't have to."

"Good. Then I will help you," I said. "And we will do it in such a way that we win, even if we lose."

First we had to go through the channels of the university. There weren't many then, except for the provost and the chancellor. No one in the administration would reverse the dean's decision. That's when I learned that superiors generally support their subordinates publicly even when they know they are wrong.

After that we had to submit the case to the Equal Employment Opportunity Commission, the Federal agency that oversees discrimination laws. The EEOC refused to consider the case—we learned later that Clarence Thomas was head of that agency at the time—but we had to go through that procedure as a prerequisite to filing the case in federal court.

In choosing a lawyer, we were determined to get the strongest attorney in town who was not afraid of Vanderbilt. After consultation, we chose George Barrett. I don't remember exactly when the case was filed in the Federal Court for the Middle District of Tennessee, but the judge was Clure Morton. On the day we filed the lawsuit, Vanderbilt announced it would establish a day care center on campus—something we had been advocating for over a decade. That was our first victory.

After many depositions and what seemed like a very long time, Judge Morton ruled against us. That was the day, so I heard, that the chancellor called the dean to instruct him to appoint a full-time director of Women's Studies, a position we had been lobbying for since the origin of Women's Studies in 1973. Another victory.

Then our lawyers appealed the case to the Sixth Circuit Court of Appeals in Cincinnati. In 1984 they affirmed the district court's ruling. The Appeals Court's judgment ended the lawsuit.

At every level of Elizabeth Langland's case, from the English department's decision to that of the federal Court of Appeals, every vote was cast by a male.

* * *

Here is some of what we learned along the way. The following list of ten is not in order of importance, except for the first three. They are all—so to speak—interwoven.

(1) Organize

What the dean could not have known when he delivered his decision that fateful Saturday morning was that we were ready and waiting. We had lost five key women from various positions in the preceding year. Further, in the ten years since I had been hired in 1971, thirty women had come and gone from the faculty of Arts and Science, leaving Vanderbilt either because of negative tenure decisions or because of discouragement that they would never even get to that point. Faculty and staff women had been meeting informally throughout the year to discuss these disturbing issues, sometimes conferring also with the two or three women on the Board of Trust, and we already had scheduled a meeting for the following Monday night.

In organizing anything the first task is to identify the cause clearly and name it accurately. We knew from the beginning that we wanted to change the status of women at Vanderbilt. Our purpose was never simply to "Support Elizabeth Langland." None of us, including Elizabeth, ever saw it that way.

We were fortunate to have a name already at hand. WEAV stands for "Women's Equity at Vanderbilt." It was suggested by a description Plato gives of the ideal ruler as one who weaves together the body politic—"the type of character fitted for the task of weaving together the web of state" (*Statesman*, 308d–311c). All strands must be included to ensure the fabric is strong.

At that Monday night meeting two days after word of the dean's rejection, we made a list of the forces most likely to influence the university. We recognized five: publicity, alums, money, federal agencies, and the federal courts. We pursued all of them relentlessly.

That night we made another decision, of which I am very proud. In our organization, staff and faculty women would always have joint leadership roles. It was the first time at Vanderbilt that the two groups had worked together on equal terms. This collaboration spread throughout the campus. Soon we learned that the secretaries knew more about what was really going on than the faculty did. From the beginning we met regularly, usually on Wednesdays at noon. We began publishing an attractive newsletter, always printed on 100 percent bond paper. Catherine Snow insisted that if we were going to do it, we should do it with style.

We knew, too, that we were working in a noble tradition: In 1920, thanks to the work of noble women and supportive men, Tennessee had become the thirty-sixth and final state necessary for the passage of the 19th Amendment to the U.S. Constitution, giving women the right to vote. Following one of the suffragists' examples of fundraising, we hosted a silver tea in which attendees contributed silver coins to the cause. We wore yellow roses, as they did, as a sign of our support.

We also organized a "Carrie Chapman Catt Day" on campus. The great suffragist leader Carrie Chapman Catt had spent six weeks in Nashville organizing the final push for the vote on the 19th Amendment in the Tennessee legislature. The Amendment passed by a margin of one vote. WEAV's honored guest that day was Claudia Bonnyman, whose great-grandfather A.H. Roberts was the Tennessee governor in 1920. After the legislature's vote, it was he who signed the certificate of ratification that ultimately changed the U.S. Constitution.

Throughout our efforts, countless allies, including many men, came from all quarters. Dean Walter Harrelson of the Divinity School was a constant friend and advisor. When a member of the administration said to him "You are being used by these women," he responded, "I am here to be used." Don Welch and Frank Wcislo appeared on a panel sponsored by WEAV featuring fathers who were significantly involved in child-rearing. C. M. Newton, Vanderbilt's superb basketball coach, was friendly to our cause, and we decided to ask him to host an educational gathering at his home. Darrell Ray, the campus Presbyterian minister, came to me and said, "Let me ask him for you, Susan. You've had enough defeats."

(2) Publicize

Carrie, do you remember the scene in the movie *Gandhi* when Gandhi asks the UP correspondent Vince Walker—played by Martin Sheen—to cover the Great Salt March? In a cause of any importance, that's what we do. We wait for, welcome, and, if necessary, invite publicity.

One of the first things we realized was that women who attended Vanderbilt in the fifties or earlier were strong and smart individuals. In those years only women applicants had to take the Scholastic Aptitude Test because only one woman could be admitted for every four men. Even when I arrived in 1971, the ratio required that three men be admitted for every two women.

These alumnae women, especially Martha Warfield (class of '48), became our strongest supporters in the community. They got together with their friends, and over the course of three years several sponsored a total of thirty-four "educational gatherings" in their homes. Initially, Elizabeth and I would go to speak about the situation of women at Vanderbilt and what we hoped to do about it. After Elizabeth left for a stellar academic career, I often went alone.

Publicity is not limited to newspapers, but in those days the newspapers helped. You may remember that one Sunday as our family was driving back to town from the farm, we stopped at Tubby's in Vanleer to pick up a copy of the *Tennessean*. Sure enough there was a big story about the Langland case on the front page of the B section. Below the headline were two quotations—one from Susan B. Anthony and one from Susan F. Wiltshire. I don't remember what I said in the quotation, but I do remember what Ashley said to me later: "I'm sure there were many reasons for you not to change your name when we married, but I'm proud you did."

On a New Year's morning in the middle of the case, I received a call from Will Campbell. "Susan," he said, "I've been looking around for a little trouble to get into, and I don't see any better trouble than what you women are doing over at Vanderbilt. Here's what I'm going to do." He said we needed national publicity. He didn't stop until he got it: a story by Frye Gaillard in the *Nation* magazine. I learned that day from Will never to ask "What can I do to help?" Just go ahead and do it.

We made T-shirts too. They were a dark green with the gold letters WEAV down one side, and across the front "WEAV EXPECTS ACTION, VANDERBILT." We wore them during a corporate-challenge run in Nashville, and the *Tennessean* printed some nice photos of our team.

(3) Raise Money

There are two reasons to raise money for a good cause.

The first is that you will need it. In our case, we needed it initially to support our publicity campaign, including buying that lovely cream-colored 100 percent bond paper. We also rented a mail box at the Acklen Station Post Office. We were scrupulous about not using Vanderbilt's campus mail for our purposes, which meant we bought lots of postage.

We also needed to pay the filing fee for our IRS 501(c)(3) status as a tax-exempt charitable organization. An endearing thing happened after we appeared before the local Charitable Contributions Board to request our Metro permit. Joseph Sweatt was the chair of the Board at the time and asked us some rather stern questions. The Board approved our request. As we were leaving, Joe came up to us in the hall, smiled and said, "Good luck. I used to work at Vanderbilt. It's about time."

Finally, we suspected we would be funding a lawsuit.

The second reason is more important. When people contribute financially to a cause, they buy into it and are invested in the outcome. The relationships made in asking for contributions also help build a strong community around one's purpose.

I have many happy memories of people who gave money to WEAV. The first person to contribute was Tom Brumbaugh, a kind professor in Art History. Sometime later he told me that he was gay. It pleased me that his was our first contribution. I remember going to a secretary in the Divinity School to tell her what we were doing. She pulled out her wallet, gave us everything in it, and said, "I have been waiting twenty years for this." Another friend calculated how much money she had spent on new living room furniture and gave WEAV the same amount. A single mother in a staff position pledged $1,000. We even received a contribution from an official in the Reagan administration. [I never added that the contributor was my brother John.]

One day two of us went to call on Mary Jane Werthan (class of '27), a member of the Vanderbilt Board of Trust. Legally, the Board of Trust was the ultimate defendant in the lawsuit. We asked her if she would help us raise $5,000. She smiled and said, "I'll try." One of the contributions that meant most was one we didn't ask for or know was coming. A check for $500 arrived in the mail one day with a note from Anne Roos, saying that another check in the same amount would be coming soon. [Later, it was Anne Roos who taught me the two requirements for getting something done: widen the matrix and raise money.]

We held one major fundraiser, a benefit concert at Langford Auditorium featuring Riders in the Sky. Catherine Snow organized this endeavor and saw to it that we sold tickets in advance. That's when I learned one should never simply set up an event and hope people come. Knowledgeable planning, in this case supplied by Catherine, comes first. The auditorium was nearly full. For the finale, the Riders sang "Home on the Range." I never thought of "Home on the Range" as a movement song, but it is. Spontaneously we all stood up, joined hands, and began to sing "Where seldom is heard a discouraging word / And the skies are not cloudy all day."

In all, we raised about $60,000.

You contributed, too, Carrie. One day you came up to me in the kitchen with a bill in each hand. "I have a one dollar bill, Mommie, and a five dollar bill. I can't decide which one to give to

WEAV." You thought a moment and said, "I think I'll give my five dollar bill, so they'll know I really mean it."

(4) Expect Insults

There will be insults. I heard some face to face. Others were reported to me. Remember, it takes two people to break your heart: One to speak ill of you, the other to bring you the news.

Several times I heard "You have a good issue, but this is not a good case." The answer to that one was easy: "I don't take bad cases." The dean of the business school said to me: "I've asked around about you. You are a good teacher and a leader, but you are no scholar." What that had to do with the Langland case I'm not quite sure, but it did hurt my feelings. For a while.

The college dean insulted all of us when he was quoted in a local newspaper as saying that research in women's studies is not real scholarship.

Then there was this: "I don't know what Susan's complaining about. She's had a lot of advantages here because she's a woman." If that had been said to my face, I would have replied: "This is not about me."

The ugliest insult came in a meeting of the faculty senate. Elizabeth was elected to the senate after her negative decision, and I was already on it. We usually sat together. One day an older woman, a professor in the medical school, rose to speak. Her father, a former chair of the Vanderbilt Board of Trust and editor of the evening newspaper, had a long history of terrorizing dissenters.

She began poignantly enough. She said that if anyone wanted to know about discrimination against women at Vanderbilt, they wouldn't believe the things that had happened to her at the medical school. Then she turned toward Elizabeth and me and said, with anger on her face, "You women, quit whining.

94

You make me ashamed." Maybe there was only a scattering of applause in the room, but it sounded like a thunder roll.

That made me mad, but another incident troubled me more. A staff woman, an editor of a campus publication whom I admired and considered a friend, said to her assistant who passed it on to me: "Susan used to have such good judgment, but she's gone off the deep end about this." I called Will Campbell about it. "The deep end is for grown-ups," he said. "The shallow water is where the kiddies play."

(5) Fear Not

Courage is not a gift endowed at birth. It is habit earned by practice and by observing the courage of others. I have heard that the words "Fear not" appear fifty-six times in the Bible. I have not counted them, but I do know that only those without fear can be generous.

As far as I know, none of us actively involved in WEAV was fearful of personal or professional repercussions. I still smile when I recall Larry Diamond. Larry was a brilliant young sociology professor without tenure who circulated a petition among other assistant professors in support of Elizabeth Langland. When people asked him if he were afraid to do that, he responded, "What are they going to do to me? Not give me tenure?"

One time I did see alarm if not fear on the face of a departmental assistant—they were called secretaries at the time—who had earlier contributed to WEAV. When she learned we were filing a lawsuit, she asked for her contribution back. "You don't sue family," she said.

I had to think about that for a while. Certainly family members do sue one another, especially after a will is read. But more fundamentally, a university or any other institution is not a family. If all is going well, it may feel like one or sometimes even function as one. But it is finally an arrangement, a corporate structure that contracts for and evaluates certain duties and responsibilities.

As for myself, I do not remember being afraid of Vanderbilt. I had had some practice by then in questioning institutions, and I was experienced enough to know something of how they operate. The one thing in the academic world I *was* afraid of, however, was something Vanderbilt could neither give me nor take away: I was afraid of not finishing my book on Vergil.

Then the oddest thing happened. On the first day of Elizabeth's federal trial, because I was a potential witness, I was asked to leave the courtroom. I walked out the courthouse door, went straight to my carrel at the Vanderbilt library, and starting finishing the Vergil book. I was not afraid anymore.

(6) Know that Nerves May Fail

Failures of nerve can happen in any long, sustained campaign. The truly dramatic episode during WEAV was when Elizabeth Langland called one morning to say that she had decided to drop the lawsuit. We had been working for two years by then, and the legal proceedings and tension were at their height.

We called an emergency meeting for that night. Several of us were discussing the dispiriting options of what to do next when Elizabeth walked in the door. She stopped in the middle of the room, smiled at us, and said, "The good thing about us women is that we get our periods. Let's get back to work."

(7) Have Fun

As you must know, Carrie, having fun is not my strong suit. I have been on the serious side since childhood. I didn't gain a real sense of humor until WEAV, and that was because of the explicit effort of our friend Catherine, who made a project of me.

The first challenge to my natural reserve came when someone proposed a "Vandy Runaround." The plan was to organize a run that passed by places having special significance for women on campus. We were to place posters at key points, which included (1) the Women's Center, at that time tucked into an attic up a steep outside staircase on West Side Row; (2) the History department, where we had our first women's studies office in an oversized closet; and (3) the building where two remarkable female professors had offices in the biology department. They had senior positions at Vanderbilt because their chair, Oscar Touster, alone among all the departmental chairs in 1946, refused to fire them after the men came back from World War II.

On this run and at our rally afterwards in Underwood Auditorium, we were all supposed to blow kazoos. I didn't even know what a kazoo was. But we did it, and I did it. That's when I learned that once you've made a fool of yourself for the first time, you're free to get on with your life.

Another value of having fun is strategic. If you are laughing, it makes the other side wonder what you know that they don't know.

A time came when we were all so weary we decided we needed to have a party. We scheduled a potluck dinner at our house. Women started arriving, and you came up to me in the hall—you were six or seven then—and asked, "When is the meeting going to start?"

"We're not having a meeting, Carrie. We're having a party."

"You mean you have all these women here and you're not having a meeting?"

(8) Face Unanticipated Consequences

This was by far the hardest part of my experience during the lawsuit. It broke my heart and the hearts of many others.

There was a lovely associate professor in the philosophy department. We were friendly colleagues and worked on projects together. He had been promoted with tenure a while before the Langland case came up.

At one point during the trial, Judge Morton asked to see all the files of people who had recently been promoted to tenure in the College of Arts and Science. This professor's file was among them. When Judge Morton saw the note the provost had inserted in his file, he exclaimed angrily, "Vanderbilt is going to lose this case right now!" The evening paper reported it under the headline: "Vanderbilt professor would not have been promoted if he weren't black."

The young professor lived at the other end of the block from us. I called Elizabeth immediately to say we had to go down there. We walked up the steps and rang the bell. The professor's wife answered the door. He wasn't home. She glared at us but opened the door a little more and motioned us in.

We sat down. She said things to us so awful I now suspect she didn't mean them. She somehow blamed us for that scurrilous note. Neither she nor her husband ever spoke to me again.

One might ask the question—and perhaps many did: "If you had known what was in that file, would you have pursued this case anyway?" Our answer was "Yes." But think about it. If we *had* known, here's what we would have done: We would have gone immediately to the young professor to tell him what was coming. We would have made sure he was surrounded by friends, maybe by his whole department. We would have written a press release for immediate distribution and urged him to do the same.

And perhaps one of us would have gone to Provost Campbell to ask him why he never got any of the blame for the note he added to that file.

(9) Remember the Restroom

Think of it as a room to rest in. It's a good place to go when you need to take off your game face. If you need to cry, it's the only place to go. You can also retreat there to share confidences with a friend—just be sure no one overhears you. Or maybe you will run into someone you needed or wanted to see.

Then repair your make-up, resume your game face, and head back out to take on the world.

(10) Wear Nice Clothes

This seems obvious enough, but it was important to me to look my best during this period, especially at public events. Regardless of any effect on others, it made me feel better.

On the last day Judge Morton was trying the case, I took you out of school to go with me to his court to hear the closing arguments. You wore your pretty gray suit and little Mary Jane shoes. Somewhere we have a picture of you on the steps of the courthouse afterwards, standing earnestly by Elizabeth Langland and George Barrett.

You are a lawyer now, Carrie, and you still wear pretty suits and closed-toe shoes to court.

* * *

The following fall the College of Arts and Science gathered for its annual opening convocation. On that occasion, each department introduces the new members of its faculty. The chair of the English department stood up. "We have four new members of our department to present to you." he said.

"The first is Professor A, who comes here from Princeton. She will hold a senior endowed chair at Vanderbilt.

Professor B, an assistant professor, is a specialist in Caribbean and African Studies.

Professor C is an assistant professor and specialist in Gay and Lesbian Studies as well as Shakespeare.

Professor D comes as a tenured English professor and Director of the Women's Studies Program."

We lost the case. We won the cause.

Love,
Mom

Sophocles, Hospitality, and Sexual Orientation

Who would reject his friendship?
Is he not one who would have, in any case, an ally's
right to our hospitality? (Theseus, king of Athens, in
Sophocles, Oedipus at Colonus, *ll. 631–33,*
Fitzgerald translation)

The eastbound and westbound buses came together for
the first and only time to pose the question to Bethany
Lutheran: "Will you choose hospitality or rejection?"
(Report of the 2007 Soulforce Equality Rides: *"East Ride," p. 8)*

In the spring of 2006 thirty-three young adult leaders of Soulforce set out on their first bus ride across America to challenge the policies of Christian and military colleges and universities hostile to lesbian, gay, bisexual, and transgender persons. Their precedent was explicit—they were consciously re-enacting a dramatic civil rights confrontation in the American South. In 1961 the young adult leaders of the Nashville Student Movement set out for Birmingham and Montgomery to ensure the continuity of the Freedom Rides challenging Jim Crow segregation in the South. They in turn were following the example of Gandhi's heroic campaign of nonviolence in India in the 1940s, which also influenced a 1947 Freedom Ride into the South by Bayard Rustin and others, sponsored by the Fellowship of Reconciliation.

But the story is older still, so old it seems timeless. In 406

BCE, the Athenian playwright Sophocles at age ninety wrote about it in his last play *Oedipus at Colonus*. Old and gray, blind and disfigured, an outcast from his own city of Thebes where his two sons are quarreling over control of the city, Oedipus is guided by his daughter Antigone into the holy grove of Colonus near Athens. Oedipus seeks a place to rest and die after the troubles prophesied for him that he had struggled to avoid. Initially, he is anathema at Colonus, reviled by the local inhabitants as one whose very presence pollutes their holy place. But Theseus, king of nearby Athens, arrives, identifies with the sufferings of Oedipus, and says that having been an exile himself, he will never turn a fellow sufferer away from his land. In this gift of hospitality Oedipus finds comfort and acceptance. He reciprocates by conferring great blessings on Colonus.

Sophocles' play does invite comparison with the freedom and equality rides, but largely in its theme of hostility or hospitality to strangers. In other ways the stories are quite different, though anchored in similar principles. The infant Oedipus was left on a mountain to die because of prophesies that he would kill his father and marry his mother. Adopted into the royal family of Corinth, he heard mutterings about his status and set out to consult the truth at the oracle of Delphi. In a moment of road rage (by no means nonviolent!), he killed a stranger, in time revealed to be his father. Then he answered the riddle of the Sphinx and thereby won the kingship of Thebes with the widowed Jocasta as queen, learning only much later she was also his mother.

The Freedom Riders and Equality Riders, in contrast, knew their truths already. The purpose of their journeys was not only to discover more truth about themselves but also to live out their truths in conscious and caring confrontation with those who would reject them.

The stories of Sophocles, the Freedom Rides of 1961, and

the Equality Rides beginning in 2006, demonstrate the power of leaving one's place of exile, even if familiar, to confront rejection at its source. When one puts one's life on the line by going physically to the source, always in a spirit of nonviolence, the process of healing long-established wrongs has a chance to begin. Staying in comfort zones is death to dreams.

Soulforce was founded in 1998 by Mel White, an ordained minister, filmmaker, and former ghostwriter for Jerry Falwell, Pat Robertson, and others. After Reverend White came out as a gay man, he eventually despaired of attempts to engage his former employers and the nation's churches concerning their hostility to LGBT persons and issues. When he circulated a message to that effect to his wide array of friends, the many responses he received included one from the King Center in Atlanta telling him he was violating one of the key tenets of Soulforce: One must never give up on one's adversaries.

For White and his partner Gary Nixon, everything changed from that moment. White began extensive study of both Gandhi's and King's principles and practices, spent time in India, then turned his extraordinary abilities to establishing a nationwide organization to confront anti-LGBT policies of the religious establishments. Today, Soulforce is the modern movement most spiritually and politically akin to the civil rights movement of the King era.

Diane Nash, chair of the Nashville Student Movement at the time, has spoken publicly of the power of the workshops in relentless Gandhian nonviolence led by Reverend Lawson: "Jim Lawson's workshops were life-changing. Few people understand nonviolence. It's not just 'turning the other cheek.' It's a powerful tool for change." She summarizes:

There were three factors in our success. The first was Jim Lawson's weekly workshops. We had an excellent education in nonviolence. The second was the Student Central Committee itself, comprised of about thirty students. We operated on consensus—Quaker style. I have looked back and marveled at what we were able to do. No one ever failed to complete an assigned task. We all had to be committed and efficient, because we knew we were going to be in harm's way. Our lives depended on it. Our 'litmus test' may sound corny now, but always we would ask ourselves: 'Is this the loving thing to do?' Third, by the time of the Freedom Ride we had already had a victory: desegregating the Nashville lunch counters. We had demonstrated that it could be done, using nonviolence. We were shocked at our own power—that we didn't know we had until we started using it.

Raymond Arsenault writes in his *Freedom Riders: 1961 and the Struggle for Racial Justice* (2006): "This was the first unambiguous victory in the Deep South. In six months all the Interstate Commerce Commission facilities were desegregated. *And* this was done in Alabama and Mississippi. The mystique of Jim Crow was broken." Arsenault observed later during a 2007 commemorative occasion: "The Freedom Rides demonstrated that young people, well-enough trained and organized, could bring about enormous social change. This was new in America. It had not happened before."

Congressman John Lewis, who was an eighteen-year-old student at the time and was terribly beaten during 1961 Freedom Rides, said at the 2007 commemorative occasion of those events: "We have to continue to build pockets of the beloved community. . . . Even if it's only a half step forward. Do not violently resist the violent. The American people are too quiet. We must speak with our feet. We have to do it. Allow yourself to be *used.* Just get in the way. Just do it. We must all become maladjusted."

When the idea of a Soulforce Equality Ride for LGBT

rights was presented to Mel White, chair of the Board of Soulforce, White proposed that they make a trial run from Soulforce headquarters in Lynchburg, Virginia, to nearby Liberty University. They did, and they were convinced it would work. Soulforce Q (the young adult section of Soulforce; Q for queer or questing) started raising its own funds and soon was ready to begin. On the eve of their departure the first year in 2006, the Equality Riders met with Congressman Lewis for a blessing and a send-off. Lewis's life, according to their young leaders, provided for them three important lessons:

- The need for an expansive youth movement for social change
- The need of the gay rights movement for more direct activism
- The imperative that the goal of youth activism must always be reconciliation.

Soulforce Q staffer Alexey Bulokhov wrote of his participation in the 2006 Equality Ride:

To be a part of the tidal wave of dialogue and change sweeping Christian America has been a transformational experience which brought me closer to my family, my friends, God, and myself. I have had the privilege of comforting closeted gay students, empowering allies amongst faculty and staff, and worshipping alongside brothers and sisters in the deep spirit of love. Moreover, Soulforce Q Equality Ride has emboldened me to believe in the possibility of positive change for LGBT people in my homeland, Russia, and elsewhere. Nonviolence as a philosophy of loving resistance is the only way to change the world: one person, one campus, one community, one nation at a time.

Numbers from the first Equality Ride in 2006 tell the story:

- Number of schools visited: 19

- Number of miles traveled: 11,178
- Number of schools that worked with us to create programming: 8
- Number of schools that arrested us: 6
- Total number of arrests: 99
- Number of school presidents who dined with us: 7
- Number of school presidents who met with us: 10
- Total number of school policies changed: 3
- Total number of gay-straight alliances formed: 3
- Total number of conversations on LGBT issues: well over 10,000

The cost for the first Equality Ride in 2006 was $288,516. The riders themselves raised $294,107, much of it from online donations. Internet and cell phones, they say, offer a huge advantage in organizing. The cost for the two East and West Equality Rides in 2007 was $354,537, also raised by the riders.

Rodney Powell, M.D., was centrally involved in the Nashville Student Movement while a student at Meharry Medical College. He was closeted during that period as a gay man. One of the eight leaders profiled in David Halberstam's *The Children* (1998), Powell was the most senior member of the group and the only one to be fully involved in the struggles for both racial and LGBT justice. His leadership was—and is—notable for what the Romans called *gravitas*, a combination of inner authority and outward calm. Powell chose not to join the Freedom Rides because the dean of Meharry told him he would never graduate from medical school if he did. First as a Peace Corp physician in Africa, then with a lifelong commitment to international public health medicine, Powell now lives with his long-time partner, Bob Eddinger, in active retirement in Hawaii, where he was a leader in the state's right to marry campaign.

In 1998 in the Fisk University Chapel, a launch event was

held for Halberstam's *The Children*. Halberstam as well as all eight individuals profiled in the book were present. As the occasion seemed to end, Powell rose and said: "I want to add one more thing. I predict that someday the churches will have to apologize for their treatment of gays as they are now beginning to apologize about slavery."

Powell said later that he had not planned in advance to say this, but his witness soon led to his active involvement in Soulforce. He has been mentor to the young adults of Soulforce Q for the Equality Rides and in other ways supports their work. Powell wrote to the Equality Ride leaders:

The Equality Rides offer the opportunity to stigmatize homophobia and American society's acceptance of conservative Christian homophobia based on the Bible. We must vigorously embrace the redemptive power of love and nonviolence used by Gandhi and King. We must follow the guidelines and strategies used by the African American Civil Rights Movement to sustain massive nonviolent resistance and social protest throughout the nation until justice is achieved. We must inspire our fellow Americans who believe in equality and justice to join us and work together to expedite political and social change.

Soulforce teaches and applies the nonviolent principles of Mahatma Gandhi and Martin Luther King, Jr. to the liberation of sexual minorities. The legacies of Mahatma Gandhi and Martin Luther King, Jr. are so powerful that they have provided principles and guidelines that have taught and inspired oppressed people worldwide to understand and seek liberation from oppression through the redemptive power of love and nonviolent resistance strategies. Soulforce has created the most comprehensive understanding, codification and presentation of the principles and strategies of nonviolence that exists. [Here, Powell is referring to Soulforce principles and strategies that are available as a Web-based resource: www.Soulforce.org.]

I believe without a doubt that if Dr. King had lived to experience Stonewall he would have transformed the Stonewall activists with his visions of the power of nonviolence when disciplined by love and redemptive suffering. I believe that Dr. King would have opposed the bigotry of many Black preachers and welcomed homosexuals to the table as part of his "beloved community." I think he would have inspired and motivated the LGBT community to organize and fully utilize the forceful revolutionary social protests he first applied in the Montgomery Bus Boycott and later in the Civil Rights Movement. I believe, under Dr. King's inspiration and leadership, powerful nonviolent strategies and sustained nonviolent confrontations would have permeated the many judicial and legislative activities by LGBT organizations and groups inspired by Stonewall. His assassination fourteen months earlier silenced his voice, but not the legacy of his bold, radical strategies of nonviolent resistance for social justice and transformation of American society.

In the spirit of love and nonviolence,
Rodney N. Powell, M.D.

We begin to sense from these stories something about the meaning of "redemptive suffering." Our redemption results from our perceiving as genuine the sufferings of others different from our own. In his first speech of Sophocles' *Oedipus at Colonus*, Oedipus declares that "sufferings and vast time" have been his teachers. Now he wants to bestow grace on others.

The saving grace for Oedipus when Theseus welcomes him is that his awful sufferings of killing his father and marrying

108

his mother are finally recognized and affirmed as true.

Theseus addresses Oedipus in the grove of Colonus near Athens:

> I am sorry for you,
> And I should like to know what favor here
> You hope for from the city and from me,
> Both you and your unfortunate companion.
> Tell me. It would be something dire indeed, for I
> Too was an exile. I grew up abroad,
> And in strange lands I fought as few men have
> With danger and with death.
> Therefore, no wanderer will come as you do,
> And be denied my audience or aid.
> (ll. 556–566, Fitzgerald translation)

Later Theseus adds words that confirm his welcome:

> Moreover he has asked grace of our deities,
> And offers no small favor in return.
> As I value that favor, I shall not refuse
> This man's desire; I declare him a citizen.
> And if it should please our friend to remain here,
> I direct you to take care of him;
> Or else he may come with me.
> Whatever you choose,
> Oedipus, we shall be happy to accord.
> You know your own needs best; I accede to them.
> (ll. 556–66 and 634–41, Fitzgerald translation)

To know someone requires that we listen to what that person has suffered. This is the knowledge that redeems us from our own narrowness and bigotry. This is redemptive suffering—and we are the ones redeemed.

Another Argument for Marriage Equality

On a recent morning my husband and I, now in our seventies, were talking over coffee about church history. Suddenly I understood for the first time why my younger brother, John, said something odd to me shortly before he died of AIDS at age forty-seven in 1993.

John said: "Gay men don't like to grow old." At the time I thought maybe he was comforting me. Later I thought, "Well, maybe they worry they will not be as attractive to younger men." Now I think I know what he intended: They fear the prospect in their later years of that worst scourge of old age or any age: loneliness and the absence of conversation, the most intimate human interaction of all.

Good conversation grows out of shared experiences of family, friendships, ideas, books, travel, memories, and laughter, accumulated over a long period of time. Marriage is no guarantee of long-shared relationships, but it gives us a chance. That is because marriage is public, affairs are private.

When a status is public, our friends and families have an investment in our relationship and an obligation to help sustain it. Our civic institutions, including hospitals, schools, and social services, have obligations to us, too. As churches and synagogues begin to recognize marriage equality, they offer holy sanction to commitments of fidelity for the long run. The state, which permits and regularizes marriage in the first place, publicly declares to all concerned its legality. If we should decide to dissolve it, the state appropriately makes that costly to accomplish.

I have heard there are over a thousand legal factors that change when a person gets married. The ones that often come first to mind are taxes, Social Security, property rights and hospital visitation. The one that looms so large in my recent memory involved inheritance arrangements after death.

Typically, the most contentious matters are what unmarried same-sex couples put in their wills. Who gets the paintings? Who gets the cherished family mementoes? Who gets the silver? Who gets the insurance? Who gets the house? If there are children, who gets them? Marriage equality brings to old age the comfort of confidence about answers to these questions.

John Keats was twenty-six years old when he died. It would take a poet to know what he knew when he wrote to a friend, "Your third chamber of life will be kind and gentle, stored with the wine of Love and the bread of Friendship."

Home

Buddy Holly and Vergil

I did not grow up with the music. In fact, as a teenager in Lubbock, Texas, I avoided popular music with the same perverse snobbery that in elementary school caused me to wear the collars of my Ship 'n' Shore blouses turned down flat in back—the collars most of my female schoolmates turned up, seductively they must have thought, behind their necks.

I thus stepped way out of my self-consciously studious world on the afternoon of June 3, 1955, when I went downtown with some of my friends to see a singer they had heard about perform at the newly opened body shop of the Johnson-Connelly Pontiac dealership.

When we arrived, three scrawny boys were leaning against the far wall, guitars in tow. Eventually a pink Cadillac with the top down drove in through the open bay door. The scrawny boys played for a little while. Then the passenger in the front seat of the Cadillac stepped out, wordlessly hoisted his guitar over his orange jacket, purple t-shirt, and red slacks, and started singing and playing.

True to form, I disdained the whole proceeding, especially the screams and giggles from the audience. I stood aloof at the back of the room, ponytail resolutely still, glad that no one besides my friends knew I was there.

It took me twelve more years of education, four years of living in New York City, and twenty-five more years of growing up to figure out the significance of Buddy Holly, the warm-up act for Elvis Presley that shiny afternoon in Lubbock.

For forty years I taught Latin, Greek, and classical civilization to college students. Sylvia Ashton-Warner's insistence on using what we grew up with to help us learn more continues to be the best teacher training I ever had.

Still, it took me a very long time to put my beliefs into practice in my own writing and scholarship, especially in front of my peers. I was helped on that journey by John Goldrosen's 1979 biography *The Buddy Holly Story*. When I read about the influences on Holly, something clicked.

In the spring of 1980, in Columbia, South Carolina, at a meeting of the Classical Association of the Middle West and South, I took the risk. I was scheduled that afternoon to talk about Vergil's *Aeneid* and why it was a permanent achievement that far surpassed its own time and place of first-century BCE Rome. I proposed that Vergil took in everything around him from his rural Italian origins, practiced profoundly the skills of the poet's trade, then married those gifts to a tradition he expropriated from far away: the *Iliad* and the *Odyssey* from Homer's Greece.

Then I paused, took a deep breath, and took the leap.

"It's what Buddy Holly did," I said. "He took in all that country music he grew up with around Lubbock, Texas, he practiced his music all the time, then he crawled into his daddy's car late at night to listen to radio broadcasts of black music from Louisiana. He put it all together, and that's how he helped invent rock 'n' roll."

Having never heard any of my scholarly colleagues say anything as down-home as this, I sat down right away. When I looked up timorously, I was surrounded by a crowd, a veritable gaggle of bald heads, old, respectable bald heads—all of them raving about Buddy Holly.

"I've been a Holly fan all my life," said one, whose years made the literal statement impossible. Said another, "I made a pilgrimage all the way from Saskatchewan to Lubbock, Texas, to visit Buddy Holly's grave." "Are you really from Lubbock?" asked a third, wide-eyed. I smiled demurely.

In that moment I came to understand the full measure of Buddy Holly's creativity: the courage to honor one's own legacy, hone the required skills, then gather into it the unknown, untried and strange in order to invent something new.

Buddy Holly had the careless courage of assuming that nothing was necessarily beyond what he could do. I don't know which example of his grinning gumption I admire more: his asking his parents to invite the outrageous Little Richard home for dinner (they finally compromised on a backyard barbecue) or his request of his older brother Larry for a thousand dollars.

Philip Norman reports the conversation between Buddy and his brother Larry, the one who knew him best, as recounted by Larry himself:

He came to me and said, "Larry, I know good and well I could make it if only I had me a decent guitar and some decent clothes." I said, "Make it as what?" He said, "Why, make it in the music business." So I said, "Okay, how much do you need?" thinking he was going to say about fifty dollars. But Buddy says, "How about lending me a thousand dollars?"

Well, I was pretty amazed, because that was a pile of money back then, but I reckoned he knew what he was about, so I scraped up a thousand bucks from somewhere.

At the time of the unveiling of the Buddy Holly statue at the new Civic Center in Lubbock, Ed Ward, a reporter from Austin, came up to Lubbock with a friend, a Lubbock native whom Ward identified only as Joe Bob, to tour the town. On the way back to Austin, Ward asked his friend to explain why so much rock 'n' roll energy came from Lubbock. Joe Bob answered: "If you don't play football and your life isn't consumed by Jesus, what else is there to do but drink beer and ride the Loop, or if you're like Buddy and don't drink, sit home and dream that your guitar is gonna get you out some day."

Joe Bob may have been right, except about that last part.

I'll take another try at it. I propose that Buddy Holly achieved what he did because he was happy. What I mean by happy is that he was secure. He was secure first because his family always encouraged him and thought his music was a fine thing for him to be doing. That kind of security made Holly free to be generous and loyal to his friends and to his hometown, including Tabernacle Baptist Church. It made him know too that his music could make a place for him wherever he was, whether at the J. T. Hutchinson Junior High parents' appreciation night or at the Apollo Theater in Harlem.

Because Holly was secure, he was also hospitable, and not just to Little Richard. His friend Peggy Sue Gerron recalls: "Buddy Holly always said, 'I'm from Lubbock, Texas'. . . . When Buddy carried that West Texas hospitality out into the world, he made the world want to come visit his hometown."

There is more than one way to be an artist—as many ways as there are artists, because that's what art is. But it is not true that one has to be anguished to make a poem or a painting or a song or anything else.

When you are secure, you are also free to write your music out of what you know. Buddy Holly always did that, which is why his songs still resonate with authenticity. When you are happy, you don't have to leave your home and family to seek out some anonymous city. Nor do you have to turn your back on the values with which you were raised. Goldrosen writes that Holly was "fresh and new, but still lived by old rules of ambition and achievement." Holly was raised to work hard, and he never quit. He never repeated himself either. When he died in a plane crash in

1959 at the age of twenty-two, he had recorded over fifty songs of astonishing variety and had written many of them.

My scholarly colleagues in South Carolina that day asked me the question, "Did you *know* him?" I had to answer, "No."

I might have met him, it turns out, because Holly used to play around at our house on 21st Street with my older brother, Davis—his 1955 classmate at Lubbock High—but that ended in junior high when my football playing brother decided Buddy wasn't cool because he played music instead of sports.

I know Buddy Holly now. But unlike Holly, who did not have to leave Lubbock to learn it, I had to journey far and long to figure out the marriage of familiar and strange that is the essence of creativity.

Two Years at Fisk University, 1969–1971

I came to Nashville in August of 1969 without a job. I had a Ph.D. from Columbia University and two years of teaching experience at the University of Illinois at Champaign-Urbana, but I had left a tenure-track job to become a law wife in Nashville. My call to the Woodrow Wilson National Fellowship Foundation from a pay phone resulted in the most fortunate event of my academic life. I learned about a vacancy and a few weeks later was hired as Director of the Honors Program at Fisk University.

My education at Fisk began when I went to the orientation for new faculty members. There they all were, seated at the head table—the president, other administrative officials, deans, and several department chairs. I looked at them and thought, *They are all educated as well or better than I and are more experienced than I am.* They were all black.

I grew up in a smallish Texas town—though any other town in Texas or in the entire South would have been the same—where I had to ask my mother what color was the water in the "colored" fountain at Sears Roebuck. Though the horizons of the land were wide, my social horizons by law and custom were narrow. For a long time I thought I had been the fastest girl in the forty-yard dash on the playground in the sixth grade in Lubbock, Texas. Much later I came to understand that due to segregation I was only the fastest white girl. At my large state university in Austin, blacks were not allowed to play any sports, work in the library, play in the band, get a haircut, or go to a movie theater adjacent to the campus.

My education, in short, had been severely stunted.

From the little bungalow Ashley and I rented in Nashville, it was 3.1 miles north to Fisk. Each school day I passed Vanderbilt University, crossed West End Avenue and then Charlotte Avenue into North Nashville, went by Meharry Medical College (which up to that time had graduated 82 percent of the black doctors in America), turned right on Jefferson Street and then into the parking lot behind Jubilee Hall, where the Honors Center was located.

Because I had been hired also as an assistant professor of English—Greek and Latin had not been offered at Fisk since 1940—my first class that semester was in World Literature. The students gathered. A young man wearing shades and hostility slouched into the back row and said audibly, "I don't think I should have to walk into a class at this school and see a white face at the front of the room." At that moment, I could not have agreed more.

Another student asked, "Why are you teaching here anyway? Are you trying to help us?" I replied, "I am here because this was the best job available to me in Nashville, and I was lucky to get it." "Oh," she said. "In that case, I guess it's OK."

It was more than OK. It was the onset of a searing season of breaking and planting, reaping and weeping (though never in front of students), risking and discarding, gritting my teeth, and grafting new stock, over and over again, onto the ragged self of who I thought I was.

But day led on to day, and in time I settled into a good working relationship with the extraordinary students in the Honors Program. They are still vivid in my mind.

Claire Patrice Sams from Montgomery, Alabama, was one of the three smartest students I ever taught in my forty years in the classroom. She first caught my attention when she overheard me grant an extension to a student who wanted more time to write her paper. Claire looked straight at me and said, "That's not fair to the rest of us who did it on time." From that day forward, I never granted an extension unless it was offered to the entire class.

Over the Fisk years and later, I grew close to Celeste Jones. One day I mentioned to her that my great grandfather had walked from Georgia to Texas behind a covered wagon after the Civil War. She responded quietly, "My great grandmother walked from Atlanta to Memphis to Mississippi and back to Atlanta to gather up her children who had been sold into slavery."

One day a gentle young woman named Charlotte Kennedy exclaimed loudly, "There's a wasp in this room!" Oh dear, I thought, it has come to this. Then I saw the wasp buzzing over by the window. Fortunately, that was not Charlotte's only contribution. One day she announced that she was going to visit the Hermitage, the home of Andrew Jackson just east of Nashville. Another student, Talmadge Guy, challenged her, "Why do you want to see where our ancestors worked as slaves?" She replied, "To appreciate their labor."

And oh, what an affirming day it was when the Honors Council was interviewing students for admission to the program for the next year. The last interviewee was a white exchange student from Carlton College. When he left the room, Walter Searcy looked around at all of us and said, "Now that all of us in the room are black again, what do you think?" I smiled.

Then there was Barton Harris, a pastoral soul who became a longtime minister in Nashville. Fisk had a January program in which students devised their own projects along with a faculty member. Barton and some others came by to ask if I would help them with a project on the black church. I told them that although I attended an interracial Methodist church, that's all I knew about the subject and they would have to educate me. We agreed, and every Sunday we attended a different church while reading black theology during the week. At the end of the month the students compiled a book of their final essays. Barton wrote the introduction. He added at the end, "It must be said that our group had no head or leader as such, but Professor Wiltshire kindly accepted her lowered status as just another nigger in the group." It was the nicest compliment I ever received.

In the second year, the Student Life office at Fisk organized a retreat in the form of a T-Group. I did not know then or now what a T-Group is, but I decided I ought to go to support the effort. We gathered that morning on the steps of the Student Center. At the back of the group was a young woman—I do not remember her name—who hated me. I usually do not use that word, but she did hate me and was furious that I was there because she did not want a white person in the group.

Later that day, we participated in an exercise in trust, in which the group, interlocking arms, formed a ring around the person in the center who was supposed to fall into the ring and trust for the best. Each person took a turn. When my turn came, I took a breath, closed my eyes, and fell face forward. I was caught safely. The leader told me later that I was the only participant who fell face first.

At Fisk I learned to lobby the Tennessee state legislature. Representative Larry Bates from Dresden, Tennessee, had introduced House Bill 20 that would require the sterilization of women who received help for themselves and their children under the Aid to Families with Dependent Children program. Though the program benefitted more white families than black, the racial implications of Larry' Bates's campaign were obvious. Celeste Jones and I decided to get to work. Three of the great women of Nashville—Jane Eskind, JoAnne Bennett, and Molly Todd—taught us how to track a bill and told us which legislators to talk to and how to approach them. Timidly, we knocked on the door of the legendary House leader, "Mr. Jim" Cummings. He smiled when we told him why we were there and said impishly, "You mean the bill of Master Bates? I think we can take care of that." The bill did not pass.

The Honors Program had a budget for travel. One weekend I went with a group from our Honors seminar studying urban issues to Chicago to attend a Saturday morning meeting of Jesse Jackson's Operation Breadbasket. Jackson was in fine form that morning, and I watched with admiration as he switched back and forth on a dime from the king's English to street patois. What impressed me most that morning, though, was when the time came to pass the collection plates. At the end, the collectors looked at the plates, signaled to Jackson, and he boomed: "We didn't get enough, so we're going to pass the plates again." Oh, so that's how you do it, I thought. Ask more, give more.

The Honors Program also had funds to bring speakers to campus. The most memorable of these was Herbert Aptheker, secretary of the Communist Party USA. His visit was a direct response to the Cambodian "incursion" of April, 1970, when American forces expanded the Vietnam War into the neighboring country. Aptheker explained that "sometimes we have to go out on the hustings when things get this bad." Aptheker was also the literary executor of W. E. B. DuBois, a Fisk graduate of 1888, but he had never visited Fisk before and long had wanted to. He told us that DuBois "was a genius, like Lenin or Goethe." I certainly had never heard a comparison like that before. Nor had I entertained a Communist at my dinner table until a group of students and I ate Kentucky Fried Chicken with Aptheker at my house.

Sometimes when I hear people refer to "the sixties," I ask them which sixties they mean. The first years of the decade were the years of the "movement," led by black churches and fueled by prayer, community, courage, and relentless nonviolent resistance.

The Nashville sit-ins and freedom rides, led by students from Fisk, Meharry, and American Baptist Theological Seminary, happened before my time, but I was introduced to them in absentia by Marian and Nelson Fuson, faithful Quakers who had been at Fisk for many years and had sheltered them all. They told me the story of the trainer of the activists in non-violence, the Reverend Jim Lawson, who had spent time in India learning about civil disobedience. Lawson usually did not go on the sit-ins because he was needed more outside of jail, but during one very tense time he did go. The purpose that day was to integrate a Morrison's Cafeteria on Nashville's West End Avenue.

All the participants were on their knees praying outside the cafeteria when a white man leaned around Lawson and spit in his face. Lawson looked up and asked the man if he had a handkerchief. The man was so surprised he reached into his pocket and handed Lawson one. Lawson wiped his face, handed back the handkerchief, and said "Thank you."

The latter years of the decade when I was at Fisk were the years of anger, rage, fire, and Black Power. Those conditions came home in a dramatic way in the spring of 1970 as we were holding the annual Honors Banquet at the Student Center. First we heard sirens coming toward campus, then commotion. Then across the lawn we saw a classroom building burning. I will never know for sure if we did the right thing—my sense is that we did: We continued the banquet while the building burned and the chaos continued.

Toward the end of my second year at Fisk, I received a call from the chair of the Classics Department at Vanderbilt. He said they had had a resignation late in the year, and he asked if I would come for a year's replacement until they could hire the right man for the job. I told him thank you, but no, I had a good job with the possibility of tenure, and I would not consider giving it up for a one-year appointment.

I was not insulted. I did not think discrimination. I did not resent Vanderbilt for wanting to wait for the "right man." All of that would come later. For now, nothing registered except that Fisk was an exciting and purposeful place, and I would not trade that for a one-year appointment anywhere.

I do not know what happened in the intervening days, but about a week later the chair called again, telling me that the department was ready to offer me a regular tenure-track three-year appointment. I told him I would think about it. It was not an easy decision.

When I received the offer from Vanderbilt, the first thing I did was make a list of pros and cons. I made sure the two columns were the same length.

Still, two large questions remained.

The first was the easy one. For me Greek and Latin literature and culture had long been the mainstay of my imaginative life. I like the languages, and the ideas and culture of antiquity seem for me like pylons supporting both a launch pad and a place of return. I know that my interests are varied and that the Classics provide a framework for sustaining them.

The other question was far more complex, and I sensed my response to it only instinctively at the time. It had to do with white guilt. I already knew that slavery in the ancient world was not connected with racism. One became a slave by losing a war. Color racism started with the Atlantic slave trade in the fifteenth century. Are all white people today still guilty of that? Abraham Heschel, the prophetic scholar of the biblical prophets, answered that question: "Some are guilty; all are responsible."

This was the era when challenges started coming from black people to white people: "Go home and put your own house in order." At first this was hurtful. Many white people over the years had risked their ease and sometimes their lives to confront racism in the South and elsewhere. But while the spirit of demands to "go home" was often not kind, the wisdom was right.

It is a hard path down that birth canal, and anyone who makes it has a right to be here. The only thing anyone can do against that is to take away or limit those rights. Black people know they have the right to vote, to live where they want, and to expect and accept the responsibilities of full legal and economic citizenship. It is white people who have curtailed and corroded those rights. That is why racism in this country is a white problem and why I needed to deal with it in my own neighborhood.

In due time I got into my little blue Volkswagen, retraced my path, and drove 1.8 miles due south to a new world at Vanderbilt University.

How Ulysses S. Grant Changed My Life

My connection with the U.S. Civil War is direct and personal. My great-grandmother Helen Hambrick Cline told my brothers and me stories about how as a little girl she hid from the Yankees under quilts while they ransacked her house in Franklin County, Virginia. She taught me to crochet and to love flowers. I was with her when she died in 1946 on my fifth birthday.

My oldest brother overlapped by two years with *her* father, our great-great-grandfather, 2nd Lt. Giles Otey Hambrick, who rode with Jubal Early in the Confederate cavalry, including at Gettysburg; survived the war without a scratch; and died in Dallas at the age of ninety-nine. Mama Cline's grandson, my father, thought "Birth of a Nation" was the greatest movie ever made. "Lee" is the middle name of another of my brothers.

My genome-bred politics changed vastly in college in the early Sixties in Austin, where I learned to stand in picket lines. "I'll meet you at the barricades," pronounced my father at a holiday meal back home. My modest activism continued—once I even went to jail for an act of civil disobedience. In 2004 and 2008 I contributed to two political books by dissident Southerners.

While in graduate school my future husband, Ashley, and I each lived for four years within a few blocks of the Grant Memorial on Riverside Drive in New York City. We never thought of visiting it. Ashley was born and raised in Richmond, Virginia, the Capital of the Confederacy, and attended Washington and Lee University where Lee served his last years as president and is revered to this day. When we married and moved to Nashville, we lived literally in the middle of the Civil War; the Federal outer defenses in the Battle of Nashville ran just beyond the yard of our home of nearly forty years on Blair Blvd. We never read the historical marker two blocks away, did not know when or why the battle was fought, who won, who the commanding generals were, or why we should care.

Sometimes the contradictions in our lives are so vast we don't even know they exist.

I finally read *The Personal Memoirs of U.S. Grant* because Elizabeth Samet noted in her *Soldier's Heart* that she read it on breaks from her graduate studies in English at Yale. *That's odd*, I thought. Also, I was beginning to hear that Grant's record is one of the best autobiographies by any U.S. president. An economist friend told me that some people believe the North won the Civil War because Grant wrote his orders so clearly. Ashley recalled his own surprise at reading Texan Larry McMurtry's admiring essay on Grant in the *New York Review of Books*.

So I checked out two copies of Grant's *Memoirs* from the local library in the small town near our farm in rural Tennessee, one for Ashley and one for me. When we finished it, I said to him, "For me this book ends the Civil War." "Yes," he said. "That and the election of Barack Obama."

When Lincoln appointed Grant in March, 1864, as Lieutenant General of the entire Union army, Lincoln was in increasing danger of losing reelection and possibly even re-nomination for the fall presidential elections. A large segment was ready to "treat" with the South, which would have resulted in a slave-owning nation on these shores and a "Union" so weakened that the European nations would have been tempted to cherry-pick what remained of it. Grant gave Lincoln the victories that saved his presidency and in the process saved the Union.

Grant begins the Conclusion of his *Memoirs* with characteristic directness and power of analysis: "The cause of the great War of the Rebellion against the United States will have to be attributed to slavery." Before the mass transit and mass communications of the nineteenth century, he explains, the various states could live secure in their own beliefs and institutions fairly independently of one another. But increasingly the South depended on the protection of slavery from Northern states and the national government with such measures as the Fugitive Slave Law.

Grant continues: "It is probably well that we had the war when we did. We are better off now than we would have been without it, and have made more rapid progress than we otherwise should have made. . . . Then, too, our republican institutions were regarded as experiments up to the breaking out of the rebellion, and monarchical Europe generally believed that our republic was a rope of sand that would part the moment the slightest strain was brought upon it."

We could have lost it all right there.

And yes, now I have learned that the Battle of Nashville was a decisive victory for the Union that hastened the end of the Civil War. The dates were December 15–16, 1864. The opposing generals were, for the North, George Thomas (like Lee, a West Pointer and veteran of the Mexican War—unlike Lee, a Virginian who remained loyal to the Union) and, for the South, adoptive Texan John Bell Hood. Thomas's victory meant the end of Hood's army as a fighting force and the end of the Confederacy's hopes for any help for Lee.

In the process of reading I discovered for the first time that 180,000 blacks served in the Union military. Many performed manual labor, but they also served in cavalry and artillery units, as well as in the infantry. One of those, the 13th United States Colored Troops, demonstrated such bravery at the Battle of Peach Orchard in the Battle of Nashville that the Confederate officer in that engagement commended *their* bravery in his battle report.

At first I felt cheated I did not know all this. I was misshapen as an American by my ignorance, and I did not even know it. I ponder what it was that cheated me. Was it because I never heard an alternative narrative growing up? Did the twenty years I spent in good educational institutions fail me? Was it because I had a sense from the age of five of who "my people" are and somehow remained loyal to them? Did I think that my more mature politics totally trumped my early sentimentality?

When we read aloud a Civil War story about Bowdoin professor and Brig. Gen. Joshua Chamberlain to our five-year old grandson, John, he interrupted: "We're for the North, right?" "Yes," we replied, with only a fleeting scintilla of ambivalence. "And the North won, right?" We nodded assent. "Yes!!" he exclaimed with an arm pump and triumphant grin.

Still, I troubled over what stories I will tell my great-grandchildren. I want those stories to be factually true—but also true to the larger story of which our own stories are only a fragment.

First I needed to do some research. A visit to Franklin County, Virginia, assured me of the facts of Mama Cline's tales. Census records of 1860 show her as two years old, living with her mother Miranda and father Giles in the home of her grandfather Otey Hambrick, a blacksmith. Further, though no significant Civil War battles took place in Franklin County, Federal cavalry raiders under Maj. Gen. George Stoneman did sweep through the area on April 6, 1865, followed four days later, the day after Lee's surrender, by a battalion under Maj. William Wagner of Pennsylvania. On raids, cavalry units did not pull supply wagons. Rather, they lived off the land, supplying their needs—perhaps also their wants—from homes and barns along the way. Mama Cline would have been seven years old when they came, just like she told us.

So for now, as to what I will tell my great-grandchildren, here's what I think I'll do: First I will tell them what Mama Cline told me, since I am one of the last of any generation to hear a Civil War story firsthand from someone who was there. Then I will tell them always to look also for the larger story behind their own.

I hope this legacy will further their learning, just as my childhood story—enlarged by an extraordinary autobiography—belatedly altered mine.

Work, Worth, and Worship

Two scriptures, one from the Hebrew Bible and one from the New Testament, speak to the problem of the relationship between work and worth, an equation that has assumed almost religious authority in American culture. The first is the Lord's proclamation to Adam after the Fall in Genesis 3:17–19: "With labour you shall win your food from [the ground] all the days of your life. It will grow thorns and thistles for you, none but wild plants for you to eat. You shall gain your bread by the sweat of your brow until you return to the ground; for from it you were taken." The second is Jesus' promise in Matthew 6:25–26: "Therefore I bid you put away anxious thoughts about food and drink to keep you alive, and clothes to cover your body. Surely life is more than food, the body more than clothes. Look at the birds of the air; they do not sow and reap and store in barns, yet their heavenly Father feeds them. You are worth more than the birds!" (NEB).

Of first importance is that these two images be taken together. One of them without the other does great violence to the realities of our human condition. On the one hand, in our broken state, we are mortal and deathly and condemned to labor until we die; on the other, we are lively, lovely creatures, susceptible to a wonderful grace that transcends those limits.

But what is remarkable about these two scriptures is that in neither of the pictures they present of our condition as human beings is work seen as something good in itself. In the first, it is clearly a curse; in the second, it is irrelevant, just as it would be irrelevant for birds to plant and harvest a grain crop.

William Stringfellow provides us with an important insight into this problem:

What has long troubled me . . . is that the inherited work ethic in this society has not, and has never had, any biblical sanction whatever. That it may be called the "Protestant work ethic" refers only to its cultural origins in white, Anglo-Saxon denominationalism in America, generically a secular phenomenon, and not to any credence the ethic has in the biblical witness. (Stringfellow, *A Second Birthday*, 1970, 61)

The equation of work with worth, in the first place is not biblical; it happens also to take an enormous and dehumanizing toll on two groups of people on our society: those who don't work and those who do. By work, clearly I mean work for pay, usually but not always outside the home. That is a fair definition because of the tendency of consumer society to consider only paid jobs as "real" work and further, to measure the relative value and status of work according to the dollars attached to it.

Who are the people who traditionally do not work for pay? The first two categories are profoundly important and numerous in our society—children and the elderly. Members of other groups (racial, gender, age, etc.) have historically been discriminated against in employment. Then there are those white women whose traditional role has been in the home (minority women in America having always been expected to work outside the home). Others are artists who are not paid for what they create, and those whose disabilities preclude employment.

Taken together, they represent the majority of people in our culture. If we persist, even subtly and subconsciously, in accepting for ourselves and others the equation of work with worth—if we believe deep down that we are only as worthy as other people think we are and that the sure sign of what they think is the kinds of work they will pay us for and how much—then what are we saying about the worth of more than half of all of us?

An artist friend in a letter to me poignantly expressed the dilemma:

It's damned hard to go on believing in yourself when you're not able to be economically independent from the work into which you pour all your intellectual, physical and emotional energy. Sooner or later you just assume that you're a failure at it or it would be affording you a living. And if you've based your life on that idea that whatever you do ought to be worth doing and the public assessment appears to be that it isn't worth it, . . . the natural conclusion is that either you should find something else you can do well enough to convince others and yourself of its value, or you are a hopelessly nonfunctional adult in our society—a washout.

She goes on to describe how the dilemma of feeling worthless anyway is exacerbated by living in some proximity, as most of us do in one way or another, to those who are doing very well by conventional standards of success: "It's tough as hell to live with or be surrounded by people who are doing quite well by Madison Avenue values . . . without either surrendering control over any decision counter to those who have social and economic power or falling prey to the idea that you're helpless or a failure vis-a-vis their values and criteria for success."

This equation takes a toll on all those who do work for pay, perhaps especially for those in the so-called "helping" professions. We know that those people wholly involved in the crass world of commerce are running after Mammon, but we can consider ourselves exempt, we tell ourselves, because we are helping people, after all, we teachers and child-care workers and nurses—and of course we really don't get paid that much anyway.

In his *Confessions of a Workaholic* (1971) Wayne E. Oates wrote the classic exposé of the perversion that results from equating the work one does with one's ultimate worth. Work

132

becomes all-consuming when we buy into the belief that success, achievement, and even mere activity are "virtuous," and that failure or lack of achievement or inactivity are "sinful"—or, if that word gets in our way, then something like "useless." Oates identifies the symptoms of a work addict as these:

- An insistence on going to work early or staying late or both, frequently coupled with the need to talk about how much we're working
- Comparing how much work we are able to get done with that of someone else
- An inability to say "no" to people who want our services or time, assuming that no one else can do the job as well as we
- Relegating emotional responsibilities not related to our job to other people so that the one all-consuming need for work can be more easily fulfilled

In one of his classes Oates asked his students to describe the qualities of their parents. Those with parents who were work-addicted responded with words like preoccupation, haste, irritability, and depression. Oates suggests that modern popular religion has made the traits of a workaholic a sort of religious, though not a Christian, virtue. The way for the reform of a workaholic, according to Oates, is paved through a rich inner life of contemplation, through which we filter what really is important and unimportant for our lives. (Oates, 12-13)

Whether we work for high pay, low pay, or no pay, all of us have the need to feel worthy. These needs include the following:

- the need for structure and a routine to give order to our lives
- the need for close peers who recognize us for the unique persons we are and provide us with support and discipline
- the need to do something visible and public

- the need to be creative and adaptable to new demands made on us, not always doing merely repetitive tasks
- the need to be involved in some way with the care of institutions, to nourish the structures that give us continuity and a sense of history
- the need for moments when we are taken completely outside ourselves, when we are lifted above both pain and pleasure, absorbed in a world beyond our own.

It happens that these six conditions, necessary for mental health, also happen to be six characteristics of worship. Structure and routine become an analogue for the ordering framework that worship provides; we talk about an "order of worship." The need for peers becomes the need for community. The need to be visible and public corresponds to our need to gather together for community celebrations. Creative adaptability speaks to the changing nature of our prayerful confessions and concerns. The care for institutions is a way of speaking about the structures that have raised us up and brought us this far as a people. Finally, self-forgetfulness is a synonym for transcendence.

A scripture in Genesis earlier than the one above describes the function of work in Eden before the brokenness symbolized by the Fall. In Genesis 2:15 we are told that the Lord took those whom he had created and put them in the Garden of Eden to till it and to care for it, charging them to make fruitful what the Lord had begun. God created us to be co-creators of the world.

House Dreams

Apparently dreams about houses are not uncommon. Generally, dreams are of no interest to anyone except contemporary Jungian analysts and the person having them. As soon as I hear anyone except Martin Luther King, Jr., talk about dreams I glaze over because I know they did not really happen and have nothing to do with me. I have been curious, however, about why I have had dreams about houses throughout much of my adult life.

The first three instances I recall were in a sequence. It took me about a decade to write my first book, a scholarly work on Vergil's *Aeneid*. By scholarly, I mean it has real footnotes. For a number of reasons this was very hard for me—I will pass over the fact that I was raising two young children and a little Cain at my university during that time—and I struggled.

Early in the process of writing the book I dreamed of a nice two-storey house down 21st Street in Lubbock where I grew up. The house belonged to someone I knew but not well. Somehow I was on the second floor, which was a disaster area. All the parquet flooring was popping up, the two-by-fours were falling in, and everything was in shambles. I was aware that if I wasn't careful, I would fall right through a big hole in the floor. It was scary.

About three years later in the process, I dreamed of a duplex somewhere in East Nashville, the city where I then lived. One of the two units had been nicely restored and redecorated, which was encouraging. Then I entered the other side that was dark, had dusty furniture stored in it, and was in a huge mess. That was depressing.

About three years after that, I dreamed I was in a lovely adobe house in Santa Fe. I walked up the interior stairwell to find a large welcoming room with walls of gleaming white stucco. A beautiful credenza stood at the far end. Sun shone in the window. Gentle reader, as you might have surmised by now—if you are keeping count and have not glazed over—at this point I had finished writing the Vergil book.

Way went on to way, years passed, and in time my husband, Ashley, and I retired and moved to our farm in rural Tennessee. We sold our house on Blair Boulevard in Nashville, where we had lived happily for thirty-five years. It was a wonderful house, built by a long-time lumber company for the owner's own home. We hosted many gatherings there, both private and public, and are grateful for all our memories of it.

Still, when the time came, that house had done what it needed to do, and we moved on without regret. When I drive by occasionally, I do not feel nostalgia, only a mild curiosity about the owners are doing to it now. I thought I was through with that house, but even after a good many years of living full-time at our farm, I have continued to have dreams, some with elaborate plots, of events happening in or around that house on Blair Boulevard. For a long time I could not figure out why.

Then I attended a retirement event for a dear friend at the Vanderbilt Divinity School. For a while I chatted with another former colleague who had been retired even longer than I. He asked me what I do these days. "Well," I said, "I read and write and help out around the farm and paint water colors and enjoy my family and friends." He responded, "I have published five books since I retired and am teaching in the retirement learning program and am writing articles and editing two series of university press books." There was more, but that is all I can I remember.

Oh my, I thought, this man is still living in his old house. Then I realized with a start, So am I. So are we all. And I realized why.

Human brains weigh about three pounds. The numbers vary, but some say one healthy human brain has something like 100 billion, others say 200 billion, neurons or nerve cells. But that's just the beginning. One neuron makes maybe a thousand connections through synapses to other neurons, which means there may be 1,000 trillion synaptic connections in the human brain. But there's still more. These synaptic connections shift and change as the brain rewires itself with each new experience.

That makes for a lot of storage space for old houses and loved ones then and now and pyramids climbed and mistakes made and gains and losses and defeats and hopes and several views of God—with room left over.

So, on the one hand, if these days I wake up from a dream about a house on Blair Blvd., I am not surprised. Instead, I might say to myself, "Good morning, brain. What synaptic surprises do you have in store for me today?"

On the other hand, I might recite the last stanza of Robert Frost's "Accidentally on Purpose," a poem I learned many years ago—by heart:

And yet with all this help of head and brain
How happily instinctive we remain,
Our best guide upward farther to the light
Passionate preference such as love at sight.

Marrying a Farm

What makes the cornfields happy, under what constellation
It's best to turn the soil, my friend, and train the vine
On the elm; the care of cattle, the management of flocks,
The knowledge you need for keeping frugal bees—all this
I'll now begin to relate. (Vergil, Georgics, Book I, *1–5)*

Vergil was a farmer. The greatest poet of Rome much preferred to stay at his farm at Nola, near Naples, than to be in Rome. He wrote a very long poem about farming, the *Georgics,* before he wrote the *Aeneid.* His father was a farmer, too. Whether I like farming because of Vergil or because of my own father, I'm not quite sure.

Where I grew up, people were considered legally married if they lived together seven years. One afternoon as I was hoeing the okra row in the garden between our barn and farm house sixty miles west of Nashville, I paused to look around at the creek, the cattle grazing in the bottom pasture, the old poplar-board house, our children playing by the porch. In that moment I knew with the certainty of a courthouse decree that I had married the farm.

Seven years earlier in 1972, after two years of weekend looking, Ashley and I had driven out to a rural county west of Nashville with a farm real estate agent whose ad in the newspaper announced sixty acres and a house for six thousand dollars. The figures were true but the sixty acres were wedged into a dry, inaccessible hollow, and the house had lost even the frames for its windows and doors.

Later as we drove along a beautiful creek, Ashley asked the agent if he knew of anything available on that waterway. I could see the agent hesitate as he speculated whether we could afford the old Della Boaz place. Finally he ventured, "Well, yes, but it's a bit more expensive."

Love at first sight happens with land as well as with people. Perhaps it is possible in either case only after you've looked long enough to know what you're seeing. What I saw first coming down the steep, heavily wooded hill was a long, narrow pasture sidling up to the road. The pasture, still green the day after Thanksgiving, seemed a welcome and a promise. My father's daughter, I noticed the fences were in good repair.

At the end of the road was Yellow Creek, wider here than where we first saw it. The house, set in a clearing of an acre or two, faced the creek. A spring-fed branch flowed into the creek on one side and a large garden plot waited between the house and the barn on the other. The barn was in good shape, too, freshly painted red along with the other small outbuildings.

The farm was about two hundred acres, more than we had wanted. Roughly fifty acres had been cleared over the years in nine different pastures, but only ten of those acres lay in the narrow bottom land bordering the creek. The rest was wooded hollows and steep ravines. When my Texan father came later to visit, he looked around doubtfully and finally said, "Well, this place isn't worth a durn for raising anything . . . except children. And it's the best place in the world for that."

The front porch of the house had rotted off, and the porch roof drooped like a drunk's eyelid. I clambered up through the front door that opened on a rather large room, empty except for a hog-salting box and a stone fireplace. Another, somewhat smaller, room with an identical fireplace proceeded from the first but was largely covered with black tar paper. Beyond was yet another small room, then a peeling green kitchen strewn with tuna cans and debris. The house had been uninhabited for several years and was used only as a hunting cabin by the owner's friends.

The house was a challenge, but by that time it didn't matter. Ashley had already said yes to the place, too, and we made an offer the next day. It took a while to find financing—the lending institutions were not impressed that the farm lacked cropland and the house lacked a bathroom—but by January the deal was closed and we got to work.

I once met a waitress at an airport restaurant who said of her work, "I've been at this job twenty-two years, and not a day goes by that I don't learn something new about it." Farming, even part-time farming, is like that. My first two lessons came on a cold January Saturday when I drove out to work with the carpenter to rebuild the porch. As I walked around the front of the house in my overalls (to my credit they were not new, nor was the old Chevrolet pickup truck we had bought a year or two earlier), Mr. Ross greeted me reproachfully: "Those aren't union-made overalls." I glanced down at the worn tag self-consciously, stammered an apology, and hurriedly got to work. Later, I learned that our county was one of only four in Tennessee that had voted for George McGovern in 1972 while the other ninety-one were going for Nixon. Somehow Ashley and I had lighted in one of the last populist strongholds in the South.

The other lesson was the larger and essential one. After Mr. Ross and I pried the drooping porch roof, piece by piece, off the front of the house, I asked him where we should drag the remains to burn them. He looked at me quizzically and told me to take off the shingles, pull out the nails, and stack the wood around back by the chicken coop. I realized then how inimical urban life is to conserving things. For years I used that wood to build various projects.

That January day was the beginning of my piecework life—urban and rural, weekday and weekend, professional and agrarian, public and private. The only thing I knew from the beginning was that I was always happy when we left Nashville for the farm on Friday and always happy to drive back to our town life on Sunday. Otherwise, Ashley and I were both filled with doubts as we struggled to raise our children, be just to our jobs and our commitments in town, raise a big garden and a growing herd of cattle, and, in my case, write scholarly articles and some books while washing dishes most of the weekend.

Dishwashing. We bought the farm at a time in the feminist movement when the dilemma about gender division of household tasks was especially raw. In the first Women's Studies course in my university I had learned something that stood me in good stead as I took up farming: statistically, men are 40 percent stronger physically than women. That fact makes not one iota of difference in a university, law firm, or urban household, but it makes a significant difference on a farm. As soon as I computed that if Ashley washed half the dishes I would have to dig half the post holes, I calmly returned to the sink. At the farm.

Our doubts about our split-up life continued to the point that more than once we contemplated selling the farm. I think we would have if it hadn't been for my brother John, who insisted we keep it ("I'll loan you the money if that's what you need"), and for Clarence and Virginia Clifton, who taught us how to farm.

When I asked Matthew and Carrie for an adjective for Clarence and Virginia, they said in unison "Nurturing." With nine children between them, none interested in farming, Clarence and Virginia took us as their own and taught us a small part of what they know and a large part of what we know about cattle, gardening, and farm life in general.

We first met the Cliftons when they rented our pastures for their cattle shortly after we bought the farm. Soon we began stopping by for Sunday dinner and good talk on our way back to

141

town. We learned that Clarence at the age of eight had watched his father killed while trying to break up a fight. As a child, his family kept the eggs they raised only on Easter Sunday. The rest of the year all were sold to support the household. Virginia was the oldest of three daughters born into her family before any sons, which meant that the girls had to clear the land themselves with a two-person crosscut saw. Virginia still had a scar on her leg from where the saw slipped one day. One year, in spite of harsh weather and being very ill, she sowed a pasture by dropping seeds in the snow.

After a year or two the Cliftons offered to sell us half their cattle with the understanding that they would continue to care for all of them. Clarence divided his twenty-eight head into pairs according to age, condition, and value, then asked us to choose one from each pair. Ashley suggested that I do the choosing since my father had won a national cattle judging contest as a student at Texas A&M fifty years earlier. I don't know whether this skill is genetically conferred or whether I remembered from Dad to look at the hindquarters, but when we were finished, Clarence smilingly pronounced that I had chosen the best cow from every pair. Eventually we bought the rest of the herd from the Cliftons, and we were on our own.

It is not quite fair to say that Ashley learned everything he knows about cattle from Clarence. In one of the early years I found him in the barn with a newborn calf under one hand and a pamphlet from the Farm Extension Service in the other. After that, however, he saved the lives of several calves and their mamas and has learned to do most of the things with cattle that need to be done. Clarence told me that when we first came to the farm he thought to himself, *Well, Ashley knows a lot about law, but he sure don't know anything about cattle.* "Now," he continued, "Ashley knows a lot about cattle and I still don't know anything about law."

John Updike says somewhere that there are two reasons to

own a farm: so you won't think heat comes from a furnace or food comes from a grocery shelf. Even though my father farmed on the Texas Panhandle and our family spent summers there, I never made a garden. Most people on the High Plains don't. Water is too scarce and the winds are too high. Virginia taught me how to plant and care for pole beans, tomatoes, onions, and potatoes, and, equally important, how to put them up for the winter. With our own beef from the freezer, whole wheat bread made of flour from my brother's stoneground mill in Texas, and frozen or canned vegetables from the garden, I put many meals on the table from what we raised ourselves.

Ashley and I bought the farm before we had children. We were thrilled when Matthew was born fifteen months later and when Carrie arrived two and a half years after that. Matthew wrote poems about the farm and made a good hand. Entrusted with the care of a sick cow when Ashley was away, he improbably got her up for doctoring by singing to her. Carrie created her own place in the woods and loved the farm cats and other animals fiercely. When asked at the age of four what the farm gave her, she replied: "Freeness." The absence of television also cleared time for reading and exploring. My father was right about the crop most suitable for this land.

We chose to settle in Tennessee in part because it is midway between Texas and Ashley's native Virginia, but that meant that we would have to raise our children at a distance from their extended families. Partly to repair that loss, we began a tradition at the farm of storytelling on Saturday nights. Everyone present old enough to talk is expected to share a story from family history or to tell about some recent adventure. A three year-old visitor became the youngest storyteller yet when she brushed off her parents' suggestions for other subjects in order to tell about the time the mail carrier found a snake in the mailbox.

We began the practice by reading from *Over My Shoulder*, a collection of my grandfather's stories transcribed by my mother. Papa Davis tells how his father as a boy, dressed in a flour sack with three holes cut out for head and arms, walked from Georgia to Texas behind a covered wagon with his family after the Civil War, and how he himself, with a third grade education, courted my grandmother with her college degree when she came to teach at a one-room school house way out in West Texas. We especially liked the story about the wolf that got caught in a makeshift range pen with a herd of cattle.

For years when friends remarked how nice it must be to have a "country retreat," I grimaced a little. The only people who are sentimental about farming have never tried it. We worked hard, especially in the early years. And if we ever entertained any notion of the farm as a private idyll, we were freed of that fallacy the first summer: overnight visitors came for nine of the eleven days Ashley and I spent on our first long stretch there. By the time we had children, we loved having company and still do. The calendar for one year shows 269 visitors, including an annual Fourth of July picnic, a church confirmation class, student volunteers from the Appalachian Student Health Coalition, a Soviet physician at Thanksgiving (probably my mother-in-law's first Communist dinner partner), a Boy Scout troop from the projects in Nashville, a small church group retreat, and all sorts of other visitors one by one and in clumps.

The farm is not a retreat from the realities of the world, nor would we wish it to be. How exposed we all are to those realities, however, is more dramatic there because at first the farm appears so remote. The Vietnam War was still lurching toward its demise when a notice posted in the one-stop store five miles away announced that helicopters from a nearby army fort would be practicing sky-hook rescue missions in the valley. Low-flying jet fighters still screamed overhead. One afternoon I saw a tiny parachute in the pasture across the branch and approached it with some trepidation. It was attached to a box with instructions to send it back to a TVA coal-burning electric plant thirty or so miles away, part of a test to track air pollution. Then there was the disaster of Agent Orange.

Some newcomer—variously identified as being from California or Texas, but apparently from Utah—bought a huge tract of land a few miles away and decided to clear it for cattle pasture by having it sprayed with chemical defoliants. The pilot hired for the job from another state chose a rainy, windy day for the spraying. When he was through, most of the valley was devastated. Many people could not put up food from their gardens that year, tobacco crops died, wells were polluted, infants got sick, and the epicenter of the sprayed area looked like it had been ravaged by a forest fire. The men in the valley gathered regularly at the one-stop store to discuss what could be done. Once when they were meeting Ashley stopped by to pick up something he needed. The talk abruptly ended when he entered the store. Then the owner said, "He's okay. He's one of us." It was a turning point.

On rare occasions, Ashley would take cases for friends in the country. His work in town as a legal aid attorney meant he could not accept fees for private cases, but the people he helped found ways to convey their gratitude. One man gave us a whole hog. Fortunately, it came with an invitation to participate in the neighborhood hog-killing. We joined in the whole process, from slaughter to sausage. Whoever said you don't want to see sausage or laws being made was wrong about the sausage.

Other social occasions help keep life in the valley green. Fish-fries and barbeques are common, as are gospel sings at the small churches nearby. Once we went to a fundraiser at the community center for a friend who had to have heart surgery. A cake-walk, auction, good-spirited arm-twisting, and, finally, bids for the leftover food raised more than $700. "It's more fun than taxes," observed our neighbor Bub. Lots of good talk got passed on at the one-stop store. My favorite was the report we heard about Cletus Smith. It seems that Cletus's wife ran off with her stepdaughter's boyfriend and Cletus's mule. Cletus missed the mule.

A guardian spirit for us in the country was Clara Pate, who had lived on the farm as a new bride for a year in 1925 while her husband put in a crop on shares. Each year daffodils still bloom in the long pasture where her house once stood. She and her husband followed the construction and engineering business around the country, finally settling in Ohio except for the years they came home to Tennessee "for the Depression." For a three-month period during that bad time, she recalls, the only money they had in the house was one dime. They kept it, knowing that it might buy a stamp if Oliver heard of a job anywhere. When they retired, the Pates moved back to Tennessee for good, and Clara Pate opened a real estate brokerage in Dickson. It was through her firm that we bought the farm and gained a friend.

Mrs. Pate was one of the smartest women I've known. She read voluminously, and when her eyesight failed, she began listening to books on tape from the state library. In her eighty-fifth year she took up piano lessons.

She was also compassionate. One grateful couple recalls how Mrs. Pate helped them buy their first place when no one else would deal with them. "You've done a lot for us," they told her, "but the most important thing you've given us is our self-respect." On another occasion Mrs. Pate forfeited her commission and worked tirelessly along with "Papa" Clement—father of Tennessee governor Frank Clement—to help an elderly gentleman achieve his dream of dying free from debt. When it became clear that his dream would come true, the old man said to Mrs Pate, "We'll both have a star in our crown for this when we get to heaven."

Mrs. Pate knew how hard it was for me to write my first book. When I told her it was finished and would be published, she said simply, "Now write one for us."

In *Bread and Wine*, Ignazio Silone shows that land can create connectedness for a life—and also that neither land nor connection can be purchased cheaply. "In our part of the world," he writes, "and perhaps elsewhere too, the relationship of a peasant to his land is a serious thing, like that between husband and wife. It's a kind of sacrament. It's not enough to buy land to make it yours. It becomes yours in the course of years, with toil and sweat, sighs and tears . . . and even when a piece of land is sold, it keeps the name of its former owner for a long time."

The latest maps of our county locate our farm at the end of "Wiltshire Lane." We know that our name, as time goes by, will give way to another. For now we are the stewards of this place, and it is home.

Poems

"A poem should not mean / but be."
—Archibald MacLeish

"A poem that do not mean, *do not be.*"
—Sterling A. Brown

First Day Out on a Long Journey

Leaning to walk, for the first time,
up the swaying gangway of a strange ship
with new mates or old made odd
in the absence of all familiar,

no hooks for hanging expectation on,
a failure of nerve descends.
Back–home anticipations, so etched and eager,
clinging to doorposts like a joyless child

in time are shaken away like water from a spaniel
pointing with determination
toward a horizon as unmarked
and receding as the sea.

Returning, Revised

The lapping waters laughed
when the master returned home at last
from gleaming Asia to gentle Sirmio.

But it was not the same Catullus
who came home to those familiar shores
and longed-for kiss of sheets—

Says one who wrestles upon return
with how to take up the threads of life
and loom she left so long ago behind.

From distant shores she brings back eyes
refracting an iridescence brighter
than the light she left.

The designs and dyes are different now,
the tension tauter on warp and woof
from all she saw in Marrakesh.

No Free Verse

(on arriving in Nauplion not knowing how to spend the day)

Would it be better to sit
in Syntagma all day,
pen poised to play,
books stacked at hand?

Or better to follow the organized plan
board the bus, see the sites
do what is right
if not what I choose?

What I choose to pursue
is the gleam in my eye
the dream on the fly
a story to spin.

But I can only write from where I've been.
Each word bears the cost
of another one lost.
There is a price to a poem.

Old and Blind, the Cyclops Polyphemus Speaks His Piece

(in pentasyllables)

"Nobody's hurt me!"
I cried, pain searing
my eye—and my heart.

Yes, I have a heart.
Your Homer mocks me
and my race, says we

Do not till the land
or send ships to sea—
Don't govern ourselves

With councils and laws.
(You can look it up
in Odyssey Nine.)

What you missed was this:
All I did for your
"civilization."

Even your bard gives
me credit for care
of my cave and flocks,

How I loved one best,

tended carefully
the needs of the rest.

You also missed this:
Do you think cities
spring full grown from Zeus?

(Surprised I know such
lore? Remember, I
am Poseidon's son.)

No, for first we need
the safety of caves.
Then we can branch out

To cultivate trees
and bees and the vine
and all else we need.

I leave you with this:
Who would you be with-
out me?

                    NOBODY.

Sex and the Barnyard
(for city folk who might not know)

The bovine genders divide easily in half.
A cow is a heifer who's had her first calf.
A bull is a male who breeds and butts.
A steer is a bull who's lost his nuts.

The equine terms are not willy-nilly:
A mare is a female, born as a filly
until she engages in sexual melding
with any fine stallion but never a gelding.

A horse and a donkey breed to make mules,
but this noble race endures different rules.
The mom is a mare horse, the daddy's a jack—
though sex is what makes them, they can't do it back.

And now for the porcines, whence comes the bacon
and sausage you really should see in the making.
The sows are the mamas of every small piglet,
while boars are those who strut by and jiggle it.

As for the goats, who do well where it's hilly,
the she is a nannie, the he is a billy.
And as for the sheep and the making of lambs
the ewes are those who consort with the rams.

I see I've passed over the wethers and shoats.
You'll need to know both, if you're worth your oats.
Shoats are weaned pigs facing lives of hard knocks,
wethers are rams who've been docked in the crotch.

Thus comes the end of this rustical ditty
meant to take sex right out of the city
and back to the barnyard, a simpler land,
where coupling is easy and wholly unplanned.

Meo Filio Aetat 1
(after Catullus)

Ludis ut passer volitans circum me.
Cum tandem te emittere erit necesse,
Tum precor ut sim, similis tibi, fili,
        Libera et fortis.

You play now like a sparrow flying around me.
When at last it will be necessary to let you go,
I pray I may be like you, child,
        Free and brave.

Launched

On her final college holiday
our daughter, latter-born of two,
prepared furiously through the night
for her first job interview.

I circled in her radius.
Why are you staying up? she asked.
You're supporting me, aren't you?
Of course, I said. I was, of course.

At the airport door she walked straight
through without a backward glance.
We watched her disappear into the crowd,
turned to one another in wonderment.

I felt scissored, as surely as
Our firstborn's start at kindergarten,
when I wandered by the office to see
if they had any counseling for me.

This departure was the final one.
The last one's leaving meant
that both had left forever
the safe familiar of our world.

For them this is continuum, their worlds
circling larger while still including ours.

For me, it was completion, a gate
I traversed at the far end of a field

I tended for over twenty years—
breaking, tilling, planting, cultivating,
weeding, protecting, fending off
the terrifying pass of storms.

What those two dear ones do not know
is that I now begin new voyages
of mind and spirit. Only a simulacrum mom
waits hopefully home by the phone.

I pause at the gate, waft a prayer
of gratitude for the harvested field behind,
take measure of the trackless plain ahead,
and slowly start the crossing.

Mentor

You will not know
the moment when
instead of seeking
you are sought.

And if you are,
you will not notice
because you yourself
will still be seeking,
seeing and sometimes
choosing the brambled
byways where lie
a lonely cistern,
cenotaph to souls
once lively there,
or strange new friend,
or poem that will
not let you go.

> Maybe, only once or more
> as you lean into a curve,
> you will catch at the
> periphery of your vision
> a younger one watching you,
> what it is you are looking for.

You Can't Marry Everyone You Love

Love endures—if I can let you go.—May Sarton

You are
The song I will not sing
The ring I will not wear
The dare I shall not choose
The music I won't know
The poem I will not write
The night I will not dream
The stream I will not cross.
So what remains from all this loss?

You are
The gleaming dance floor where I glide
The morning star that seems a guide
The shade you make I often rest in
The burnished map of where I've been.

This love more lasting than surmise
This love that's kind and fair and wise.

Lines upon Losing a Journal

Losing a passport is an inconvenience. Losing a journal is a disaster.—Robert Martins

Hurrying to leave the train at Pisa
I left behind the record of the weeks before
and grieved that with the record
all was lost.

Once the small bound book was gone for good
after all efforts failed to find it, I worried
the absence like a child the space left by a
new-pulled tooth.

The dailiness, I knew, could be reconstructed according to
       the need.
The names alone of places stayed could serve
as suns governing by their gravity whole
circuits of stories:

Astoria Nomikos Galini Kalypso Olympic Victoria
Suisse Adua Bartoli Consoli di Mare Milano, San Marco—
each a small lifetime compressed into syllables,
diamonds from coal.

But what of the dreams that graced each day
with color, raiment, shape—those thoughts that flocked
unbidden, metamorphosing slowly into meaning
as I watched?

How do I salvage those while the wind blows rain
hard against my pane in Castiglioncello
where finally I landed after a bleak diversion
through unlovely Livorno?

How it felt to circle the Martinengo Bastion of old
Iraklion where Kazantzakis lies beneath a stone that reads
"I hope for nothing, I fear nothing, I am free" but
bears no name.

And how later in that dear narrow room in Rome
at 26 Piazza di Spanga, I wondered if Nikos knew what
clear-eyed Keats demanded, that a poet's name be writ
in water only.

How at that same door in '44 the soldier-poet of
the Second War, the one descended from Archilochus,
knocked to announce "I am a student" and rejoiced
to surrender to poetry.

How my room at the Nomikos Villa was a trapezoid
wedged into the core of the volcano, widening toward
the caldera of Santorini like a birth canal from
the center of earth.

How I felt when I saw Hermes holding the smiling child
at Olympia, both of them coaxed (at what cost?)
out of marble from the mines at Paros I had visited only
a day before.

How I came to see that the corridor from the high Plains

of Texas to just south of Taos, where the air is composed
of the same humors I am—old Epicurus believed
souls are matter—

skips like a stone over an ocean and several seas to the
flat high-skied Aegean where I feel the same
primeval oneness that Parmenides said once
was true of all of us.

How Rome became at once much more like home
and so much more remote from all my grasp
that I embraced her as I might
a furtive lover.

Whom I must flee before first light, before
first pealing of the bells all round
so not to be caught lying
with a stranger.

How Michelangelo's Last judgment says no one thing
but how his Expulsion from the Garden does:
that the very knowledge that makes us human will also
break our hearts.

How I felt an uncontestable shifting of the poles from
righting wrong to writing plain, and how I wondered
which of these—or is it friends?—will matter most when
all is done.

How there were moments en route when I felt as if I were
living the story I'm writing as surely as a quilter
piecing the leftover fragments of multiple

lives into art.

How dearly I seek to convey all those characters lurking
in my brain like Michelangelo's prisoners
into a braille writ clear enough for all
the world to see.

How Michelangelo knew what Vergil knew, what so few
do, that it is possible, but only by the finest hew,
to tell the truth and please
the patron too.

How Brunelleschi's double dome's a metaphor
not for a city only but for life, the one enclosing
the vast unknown within, the other that without,
and how we,

like his laborers, traverse the narrow catwalks between
the two, their curves dizzying us always bending over,
with nothing at a distance we can see
to steady us,

Until, pausing in the endless work to steal
a bite or kiss, we catch through tiny windows
a shining glimpse of the vast round plate below
or azure bowl above.

And know then that the work is good,
even if we must soon descend the narrow curl of steps
toward the door that exits to or from the world
in one direction only.

How I asked myself if I had done enough,
become whatever inchoate thing I never quite imagined,
then heard as surely as if spoken to, *Do the work,
the rest will follow.*

How a story's end and start are always lies
because they both deny the thousand-stranded skein
that always ends later
and begins before

but how this, even, cannot divert a heart
from a journey or a poem until at last,
as Rodin said of any art,
each must be abandoned but is never finished.

To Vergil, His Birthday

I dreamed of you once—
a tall man, dark, countrified,
dressed in old black suit and fedora,
oblivious of your silence.

Months later I understood that it was you
I followed that day at the airport,
abandoning toys at the baggage claim,
dodging bullies bent on stopping me.

You passed the gate up to the plane,
I squeezed through just in time,
knowing I would follow you—
where did not matter.

You were more ambitious than your peers
but not as most Romans were ambitious.
You, who knew power,
stayed away from Rome.

You dared to compose a story
better than Homer's, public and private.
You wrote it both ways,
as a Libra would.

Your few close friends survived:
Varius, Tucca, but most of all Horace.

I hope he loved you back.
It took you both to write what each one wrote.

Three lines a day you averaged,
Were there days you did not work at all?
Were you ever depressed, hopeless?
Most of all, my ally, I ask this:

How was it when you finished?
Why did you beg others to burn it?
Was it something in the poem—
or in you—that was not right?

Did you really wonder how the wrath
in celestial minds could be so great?
I think you knew it is in our minds
where that wrath is.

Dear Vergil, when you died at fifty-one,
what was left for you to do?
After Homer you had matched the best,
told the hardest stories closest to the bone.

Could I be living on for you,
a dozen shores and more away,
unwilling to annul public,
unable to adjure private,

wondering ever how to read
the past through palimpsests.
Like you a farmer, steward of heritage,
seeking all ways to make the old new?

Your poem ends with *umbras*.
Once I found that sad. No longer.
Now I like shadows. They are companions—
bread for the journey.

Shadows change, lengthen, contract,
fade and come again,
like kindness or a friend.
What you see depends on where you stand.

Short Stories

Liza's Quilt

Liza Myatt leaned forward in her aluminum lawn chair, looking intently at Len Barker over by the sugar maple. When she saw his index finger flick almost imperceptibly the fourth time, she knew the auctioneer, Colonel Burns, only had to add the usual flourishes to his routine before the pie safe would be sold.

It was the nicest thing she had. She had bought it with her egg and butter money nineteen years earlier when the Moultons sold out. Colonel Burns had been the auctioneer then, too, and she had decided then that he would handle things for her when the time came. His auctions were a cross between an ice cream social and a political rally. He had already introduced five local candidates that day, two of them getting special notice because he used to play ball with them or their daddies. And he could sweet-talk one more bids like a preacher at alter call: "Still cheap at the price."

She was glad the Barkers got the pie safe. They had helped her since Orman went into the nursing home in Richardson nine months ago and had sent over their two boys this morning to help her move the rest of her things out onto the yard for the sale. She was so grateful for their help that she pretended not to notice when twelve-year-old Jake carelessly tossed two sterling silver teaspoons into a paper bag of knickknacks he was carrying out to the auction table.

She was pretending not to notice a lot of things today. The July heat, though she was mostly used to the heat. The size of the crowd, a little smaller than she and Colonel Burns had hoped. Mostly she was pretending not to notice the looks on people's faces when they glanced at her, the concern from the people who knew her and the shallow pity from those who didn't. They were the ones who bothered her the most, the pitying city folks who didn't know her from Adam.

You could tell which ones they were right away: the nervous way they stood, always looking around the crowd but pretending not to. A couple of men wore Co-op hats and blue short-sleeved coveralls, the kind you get for $17.99 at K-Mart in Richardson, but you just knew it was the idea of farming they liked more than the work of it. It was the women, though, that she resented the most, the kind who are nearly happy because they have nearly everything they want.

Liza had gone to enough auctions to know how it worked. The women would get a little jumpy at first and bid something too high that everybody knew was as cheap as it looked. Then they would gather themselves up and lean right into it, narrowing their eyes like a pro at a poker table. They would pass the afternoon piling up the small victories they could win here, since they couldn't even play any games that mattered at home.

Billy Mitchum, Colonel Burns's assistant, was holding up a yellow Rubbermaid dishwashing pan filled with odds and ends. Liza saw that it included her lighted make-up mirror, the only trifling thing she had allowed herself during those years and maybe the only vanity she owned. Billy had trouble getting the bidding started. He finally sold the whole batch for $2.00, but not before Liza recalled the day she bought the mirror on sale at a Walgreen's in Memphis.

That was the time she had gotten on the bus and gone to the city by herself. Orman hadn't wanted her to go off, but of course he never did. She knew that was because he was more worried about himself than about her. She had wanted to get Luke's baby shoes bronzed, and no one in Richardson could do it. That day it felt so good to be out on her own that she nearly laughed out loud when she sat down at the counter at Walgreen's and ordered a Cherry Coke and hamburger.

That was the day she realized she was no more or less alone than she had been before Luke was killed nine years earlier in the car wreck coming home from his construction job in Pulaski.

She had thought her life was over then, and for a time it was. The silence between her and Orman widened, and after a while he started talking about leaving her, though he never did. But when she got off the bus from Memphis at Newsom's Store late that evening, her heart was lighter than it had been in years. It had taken her that long to pack up her sorrow and let it be.

Now, Billy was holding up the guitar Orman gave Luke for his fifteenth birthday. It was just about the only thing that ever passed peaceable between them. Orman could never play it at all. He had bought it for himself, years earlier, at a pawnshop in Nashville around the corner from the Opry in one of the few fanciful gestures of his life. When the tobacco dried up the next year, that's all they had to give Luke for his birthday.

Luke never really took to the guitar either. But Liza leaned back and smiled to herself as she remembered the warm spring evenings when Frank Mays would come over and sit with them on the front porch. Frank had learned a few chords from his Army buddy on the ship headed to Oran in late '43, and he could put them together in a moving way with tunes he had heard his father sing.

Frank was different from other men in the valley. He paid attention to things, and he listened to what she said. When she occasionally browsed in the county library in the basement of the courthouse, she noticed his name was signed on most of the check-out cards in the back of the books.

The sun was slanting behind the house now, and the crowd had moved over to the furniture under the other sugar maple.

Colonel Burns started picking up the quilts piled on the bare mattress of their old iron bed. Liza leaned forward intently, watching carefully now.

The first quilt, a double wedding ring, sold for far too little, she knew. City people were collecting quilts these days without knowing much about them, but the woman who bought this one got a lucky bargain. The second two, twin size with a green background that Aunt Sophie had made, were in bad condition and brought about what they were worth.

Then Liza drew in her breath as Colonel Burns spread out the pieced quilt top, trying awkwardly to gather under his long arms the yellow backing and polyester batting, still wrapped in cellophane, that went with it. Quilts have three layers, but of this one only the top was finished. Liza had long depended on store-bought polyester for the thick center layer, often made of cotton in the old days, and the yellow fabric for the backing. But she never quilted the three layers together. Somehow that seemed irrelevant.

This was the only moment of the afternoon Liza had been anxious about. She knew it made people nervous to have her there, and her friend and neighbor Sally Luton had offered to take her to a movie in Richardson for the afternoon. No one except maybe Frank could have understood that the sale was oddly a relief for her. Except for the few things she had taken to the little apartment next to the nursing home in Richardson, everything she had accumulated in forty-five years of married life was disappearing this afternoon. Of what was left, only the quilt top mattered.

It was not a pattern anyone recognized because she had made it up herself. Each square had diagonal strips in all sorts of widths and angles, and every square was different. Except for the back room curtains and a graduation dress she had made for her niece, all the pieces were remnants from shirts she had made for Luke over the nineteen years of his life.

She had started the quilt a year after he died, crazy sometimes with grief and sometimes just numb. She had read somewhere that any grief was bearable if you could tell a story about it or make a story out of it. She couldn't make a story, but she could make a quilt.

When she finally finished piecing together the top, she knew she would never put the backing on it. She had done what she needed to do. Sometimes she would spread it out on the bed, sit in her rocker, and stare at it for a long part of the afternoon. A piece here or there would help her remember a detail about Luke's life she had forgotten, and sometimes the scraps in the pattern would form new connections in her memory of him. In ways she did not fully understand, the quilt top began to solve a problem for her.

When Joey Barker asked her this morning if she wanted to sell it at the auction, she paused only a moment to confirm her decision. Yes. It was time.

Instinctively, Liza wasn't sure about the tall woman standing behind the cot. Her haircut was expensive and her daughter pretty. Something determinedly sincere about her didn't settle quite right. She saw the woman eye the quilts, begin to bid on the first one, but pull back after the first round or two. She shook her head no on the twins and then picked up interest again when Colonel Burns reached for the quilt top. The woman entered the bidding after the first offer, nodded yes again after the confusion about whether the backing and batting went with it, and finally got it all for seven dollars.

Half an hour later, Liza remembered something. It touched her somehow that she had forgotten this one last thing. She rose from her chair and reached her right hand deep into her pocket as she looked around the crowd. Seeing the tall woman talking with Wilma Barker, Liza walked up to her slowly. Cocking her head just right, she looked her straight in the eye. "Are you the lady who bought the quilt top?" The woman replied yes, surprised and a little confused.

Liza drew her hand out of her pocket, extended her arm directly toward the woman, and dropped two spools of yellow thread into her hand.

"Here's what it was supposed to be put together with," she said.

Liza Myatt turned and walked away. Nobody saw the quick nod she gave herself or the faint smile playing across her face.

The Violin

The second movement of Bach's *Sonata No. 1 in G Minor* was difficult for her, a complex fugue requiring intense concentration, and she wanted to get it exactly right. Erika Howe chose to play the violin at her father's funeral because on that day of all days she wanted to be an agent rather than a witness. When her brother Harry died five years earlier, she had been too immobilized by grief to play at his memorial service. Now, as she waited, she felt as serene as the late afternoon light streaming through the vermilion panes of the stained-glass windows.

At twenty-six, Erika's confidence was hard-won. She had been playing the violin since she was five and had won her first major competition at eleven. At seventeen she received one of only six violin scholarships nationwide to Julliard. It had taken years, however, for her to arrange a cease-fire between her talent and her life.

Much of her present poise, she knew, was due to her teacher during her turbulent years of adolescence. A young widow of enormous abilities, Constance Jenson had moved from Minnesota to North Carolina to teach at the local conservatory when Erika was thirteen.

Even before she arrived, Constance had heard about the remarkable talent of this shy young prodigy. Still, she had been reluctant to take Erika as a student. Constance had never taught anyone so young, and she was aware of the potential pitfalls of such a relationship. She might push her too hard or not hard enough. She also worried about whether a too-close identification with a teacher might create a barrier between an adolescent child and her parents.

After a series of master classes, however, Constance was willing to venture the chance. Her decision was eased by the generous hospitality of Nancy and Randolph Howe. Though not especially musical themselves, Erika's parents welcomed Constance warmly into their home and their lives. The summer of Erika's sixteenth birthday the four of them took a trip to England together to hear a chamber music series in a progression of cathedrals.

Awed at first, Erika quickly came to trust and soon to love her new teacher. Constance became the attentive aunt or older sister Erika never had, even while both carefully observed the appropriate boundaries between them. Erika always called her Mrs. Jenson.

It was because of Constance that Erika held in her possession the Amati violin she so cherished. The year Erika was a junior in high school, Constance was invited to become a member of the Serafin String Quartet in New York. This remarkable move also meant that Constance would have to find a violin of the highest quality to match the standards of the Serafin.

The violin that Constance had lovingly relied on all those years had been given to her by her mother, herself a concert violinist, when she retired. It was a beautiful instrument, made in Cremona in 1647 by Nicolo Amati, the teacher of Stradivari—another case in which the student surpassed the teacher because the teacher was so good at what teachers do. Constance wished she could give the Amati to Erika, but her predecessor in the Quartet had offered to sell her his Stradivarius, and she knew that she would have to sell her Amati for at least $100,000 in order to pay for the stunning Strad.

One afternoon before leaving for New York, Constance had a long visit with Nancy and Randolph Howe. The next day she told Erika that she wanted her to play the Amati for a year. At the end of that time they would try to find a way for her to buy it.

"It's only fair," she said. "I have the use of the Stradivarius for a year, too, before I have to pay for it. Maybe we can figure out something for both of us."

Constance told her about a private benefactor on the West Coast who helped unusually gifted young musicians gain access to the finest instruments. She would send him a compact disc of Erika's performance of Wieniawski's *Concerto No. 2 in D Minor.* She knew he would be struck, Constance said, by Erika's musicality, especially the brilliance of feeling she conveyed in the third movement of the concerto.

A year later, Constance called Erika from New York.

"We've worked matters out. The Amati is yours," she said.

Erika was thrilled to own this treasured instrument with its burnished maple belly, ribs and back of spruce feathered with faint tiger stripes, and an ebony tailpiece so fine it looked and felt like polished onyx. She cared for the Amati like a mama bear with her cubs, and the fine black case in which she carried it was rarely out of her sight.

Erika's mind wandered back further. When she was in her third year at Juilliard, her world was shattered by the death of her brother Harry from AIDS. Her only sibling, twelve years older than she, Harry had always loomed on the stage as the actor whose measure she could never hope to match.

While she was still in high school, Erika had looked for psychology books at the local university library to try to figure out how two siblings with the same parents could be so different. Where she was shy, Harry was gregarious. While she worked hard to develop two or three close friendships, Harry had dozens. In any room, Harry's presence commanded attention. This seemed effortless on his part, and as she grew older, Erika conceded that it genuinely was.

People were his gift, as music was hers. She remembered the long-time family friend who asked her father at a campaign fund-raiser for Harry, "Where in this very civic family did Erika get her talent for music?" Randolph had grinned and replied, "She got her talent by practicing six hours a day."

Erika remembered how pleased she was by that. Her father's answer gave her credit for her hard work instead of explaining away her talent as an unearned inheritance. Still, she was curious why she felt so different from her parents and from Harry. In one of her psychology books, she had read that because of the way genes split, children can receive as much as sixty-five percent of their genetic inheritance from one parent or the other. Maybe, she smiled, through her mother she received a specially large dose of genes from her great-grandfather, who played the fiddle at country dances before he married his Methodist wife.

What had saved Erika during the difficult years of early adolescence was not her genes or her parents or her brother or her talent—if anything, her talent was her great burden—but the Smooth Stone.

A path led out from the back door of the cabin near Cruso through the steep valley of Wolf Creek. In the late spring the woods were laced with mountain laurel like a florist's shop. About a hundred yards up the valley, a path of smaller rocks led out into to the rushing waters of the creek to the huge rock that Erika as a very young child had named the Smooth Stone.

She loved to sit on its damp iron-hard surface for hours, wafted away on the wings of limitless possibility that children possess if they have been loved enough. Once when Nancy and Randolph asked Erika what she liked most about the cabin, she answered, "Freeness and the Smooth Stone."

Now, as an adult, Erika was still able to summon the feelings of those long, hourless days. Sometimes before a performance or a recital she would imagine herself again as a young child with straight brown bangs, wearing a little t-shirt with a sunflower on it and sitting happily on the Smooth Stone.

Erika had been hurt and bewildered when her parents sold the cabin when she was fourteen, the same year Harry ran for the state legislature. Harry had narrowly lost the race against an entrenched incumbent. Part of the problem had been the aging incumbent's thinly veiled references to the "lifestyle" of his single young challenger. She wondered if Harry might have been able to win his election during present days if he were still alive.

Nancy and Randolph Howe were both elementary-school teachers. At different times each had been asked to become a principal, but both steadfastly refused, insisting that their place was in the classroom. For them as well as for their two children, the cabin had been a place not of retreat but, as Randolph routinely replied with a smile, "attacking in another direction." That was where each of them could do what he or she enjoyed and still be within earshot of one another. When she was young, Erika had sometimes resented how much attention her parents paid to their students even outside of school hours and to their other community activities, so she treasured this time when they were all together as a family.

The senior Howes explained at the time that they were selling the cabin because Harry had already left home and Erika was now spending most of her summers at music institutes. Soon, she too would be off to the conservatory. Still, the sale of the cabin was a blow for Erika.

Today, she would not play the rest of Bach's sonata because she wanted to conclude with the energy and force of the second movement. Her first piece had been Bach's "Air on the G String," accompanied by the gifted organist on the glorious Holtkamp organ the church had bought the year before, and she chose to respond to its more somber tone with the vitality of this movement.

When she finished she stood alone at the side of the organ. She bowed her head briefly, then raised her eyes and smiled at the rapt congregation.

There before her was her communion of saints. On the first row were her inimitable mother Nancy, still trim and beautiful at sixty-four; her own husband Edward, principal cellist of the Philadelphia Philharmonic Orchestra of which she herself was principal of the second violin section; and Constance Jenson. Behind them were rows of people who had known and loved her all her life. She thought of them now as a large flock of beautiful birds who had circled around her for a lifetime, adding twigs to the nest that kept her safe and secure.

After the benediction she walked toward the first pew and bent down to put the Amati back in its case. Then she straightened her shoulders purposefully and began greeting the guests.

Eventually, everyone reconvened for a reception at her family's modest home near the university. Even though small in size, the house was filled with books and art, and people always loved to visit there. Erika wished that her parents had traveled more after their retirement, but they insisted they were supremely happy at home with their books, their friends, and each other.

David Harlan, a lawyer and close family friend who had served as Harry's campaign treasurer, came up to her.

"It was beautiful," he said. "I wept."

"Thank you," said Erika. "I was surprised how happy I was to play. I think Dad would have liked it, that I didn't just sit there woolgathering, as he would have called it."

David grinned in agreement.

"Will you have time to come by my office next week before you fly back to Philadelphia?" he asked. "There's something I want to show you."

"Of course," Erika said. "If it suits, I'll come Tuesday morning."

"That will be fine," he said.

Three days later Erika waited briefly in the simple but tasteful reception room. David walked out to greet her.

"Hello," he said warmly. "Come on in."

David reached for a file on top of his desk.

"Randolph never expected you to see this. Your parents thought you were too young at sixteen to have to worry about it, but Nancy and Constance thought this was the right time."

Erika waited in puzzlement. She could not imagine what this was about.

David opened the file, which consisted of only three pages. The bottom two were stapled together. On top was a piece of unlined bond paper, with columns of dates handwritten in Randolph's precise penmanship, each followed by the amount $1,213.54.

"What is this?" asked Erika.

"The mysterious benefactor did not pay for the Amati," said David. "His foundation only loans instruments to gifted young musicians while they are still studying. Your parents mortgaged their house to buy your violin for you. They made the payments with Randolph's pension from the Board of Education, which was $1,286 a month. The mortgage was paid off three months ago. A copy of the release is in the file."

David handed her the folder.

Erika sat in silence, her eyes fixed on the rows of figures on the page. Tears streamed down her face.

"Your parents also made a sizable contribution to Harry's legislative campaign shortly after they sold the cabin on Wolf Creek," he added.

"They told me these were the two best investments they ever made."

Kestrel

Icy rain stung her windshield, wipers at full speed. She was in good spirits in spite of the gloom, headed home to her farm in Grainger County after a happy lunch with her lawyer daughter in Knoxville and a few errands. It was late now, darkening early toward the shortest day of the year. The traffic ahead on the narrow two-lane road was heavy and slow, but she figured it was the city and university employees making their way to their homes in the country in bad weather after a hard day.

She barely noticed the first one, a car parked on the left side of the road, its right wheels off the pavement. About thirty yards later there was another one. Then, shortly after that, a third. All were in the opposite lane, headed the other way and parked with their right-side wheels off the road, headlights off. The fogged windows of her own and the parked cars prevented her seeing whether or not those cars sheltered people.

Only after she had passed four or five more similarly parked cars at various intervals did she begin feeling troubled.

This was getting creepy.

Finally, at the head of a long curve she saw blinking police lights. OK, so that was it, a wreck ahead caused by the dark and bad weather. Easy enough to happen even in broad daylight on these narrow country roads.

But what kind of wreck, and how could it explain the silent row of parked cars on her left, as orderly if intermittent as a straggling platoon of new recruits? She was moving now twenty miles an hour or less.

The silent, outward-bound sentinels on the other side of the road kept reappearing. Her imagination wandered: Was this some sort of weird used car sale? Maybe a gasoline truck had wrecked, the fumes overcoming the drivers who passed it from the other direction. With some alarm she saw a yellow school bus among the parked vehicles, side tires also off the road.

Glancing ahead for the blinking police lights, she noticed they seemed no closer. They were moving down the road. Only then did she get it: of course, it was a funeral procession, and she was in it. A city girl most of her life, she still was not used to the seriousness with which country folk did right by their dead. In town she would sometimes see a few cars pull over as a funeral cortege passed by, but the drivers always seemed bent over their steering wheels talking on their cell phones, eager to take off at first opportunity.

She was relieved finally to know what was going on. The question now was what to do about it.

* * *

The day before the burial, Wayne Collier's mother and brothers gathered uneasily around the funeral director's worn desk, sitting slantwise across a fading plum-colored carpet. John Rowe, who ran the business by himself, lowered his head wordlessly as he listened to the oldest brother's rant. "Wayne's been running around for years, drinkin' and cuttin' up, driving that red truck a hunnerd miles an hour like he owned the place. No wonder he finally ran off a road at 2:00 A.M. and rolled that bugger all the way down the hill. I say we stick him in the ground as quick as possible and be done with it."

Wayne's widowed mother winced, sharpening the features on her bony face, her darting eyes signaling her grief both at the death of her youngest son, who everyone knew was her favorite, and at the nonstop attacks on Wayne from her oldest boy. Hank Collier had been angry his whole life, taking out the abuse from his father by inflicting it on his youngest brother. Hank subsisted mostly on odd jobs for farmers around the county. He had been fired from the only two regular jobs he ever had because of his outbursts of rage.

The middle son Dave sat quietly between his mother and Hank. When Dave was coming along, he helped hang drywall at whatever jobs his father could pick up. But when Art Collier died of lung cancer, fifteen-year old Dave knew for sure he had to get out of the family drama. He chose the option of education. He had graduated from the county high school with letters in three sports and had won a scholarship to the nearby teachers college. He now taught biology and coached basketball back at his old high school.

One person was conspicuously absent from the little circle. Wayne's longtime girlfriend Jessie Harris had two children by Wayne and was pregnant with a third. Wayne and Jessie had decided to get married on the upcoming Valentine's Day and had started looking for a little house they could afford. Wayne still caroused some and had been drinking late with his buddies the night of the wreck. But he was twenty-eight now and had been settling down. He told Jessie that being a family with her and the children was what he wanted more than anything in the world, and he gave her a ring to prove it. Hank, in one more gesture as self-proclaimed head of the family, had pointedly refused to include Jessie in the dealings with the funeral home.

John Rowe broke in. "Where do you want to bury Wayne? And what do you want at the graveside service?" Rowe knew the family didn't go to church. Flora Collier murmured: "Some of Art's people are buried up on Piney Ridge Road. There's room there for another grave."

Then Rowe asked, "Do you want to find a minister to do the graveside service?"

Hank bellowed: "No! I don't trust those jockeys for Jesus a minute, always keepin' their eyes on the collection plate and lookin' out for poor old widows they can con. And they'll just have their hand out for a check at the end of the burial. I've seen 'em do it."

After a moment Rowe offered an alternative. "Actually, there's a lady down toward Knoxville from here, some sort of priest who won't even accept an honorarium. Sometimes she'll do things just because they need doing if somebody asks her."

"Absolutely not," Hank barked. "If there's anything worse than a prissy pink-ass guy preacher, it's a dyky fat-ass lady preacher lady who hates men!"

Dave asked. "What's her name?"

Rowe replied, "Ellen Alsobrooks."

"I know her," said Dave, surprised. "At least I met her once when Dad and I hung the dry wall for the addition she and her husband were making to their house down on the old Bishop place. She seemed real nice. And she cooked a pretty good lunch, too. I think I heard from one of the teachers at school that she had made a preacher."

Flora sat quietly for a moment. Then she said with a voice so firm it surprised even herself, "We will ask Miz Alsobrooks to do it. John, will you give her a call for us?"

"Yes, if that's what you want. But she'll want to talk with all of y'all before the service. She thinks about these things, doesn't just read from the *Pastor's Manual*. Could you meet her here in the office, tomorrow at four if she's available?"

Flora and Dave nodded. Hank growled: "What are we supposed to say to this so-called lady so-called preacher?"

John Rowe's smile was borne of long experience: "Exactly what you've told me," he said. "Plus anything or anyone else important to Wayne."

John knew about Wayne's fiancée Jessie Harris. She was his wife's cousin's youngest daughter.

* * *

Creeping along in the funeral line, she formed a plan. When the procession turned off, she would simply keep on driving straight.

Then another thought started forming. Maybe she would attend this burial service. It helped that Purcell's Concerto in D Minor was playing on the public radio station. She had lots of time this afternoon, probably the thing she enjoyed most since retiring from her teaching job a couple of years before. So maybe she would follow along. She had already been in the procession for a long time, and it was beginning to seem disrespectful just to peel off at the first possible moment.

The decision was made for her. When she approached the flashing police lights, she saw that two patrol cars had formed a diagonal across both lanes so that the only way to go, without pleading with the officer, was to turn right. She took a deep breath and followed the procession.

The next time she looked in her rear view mirror, she saw police lights blinking right behind her. Ohmigosh: Did she have her registration and current insurance information with her? What had she done wrong? But as the moments lengthened, she saw that the patrol car was simply following along, bringing up the rear of the procession.

Now she started worrying in earnest about what or who she would see in this small, overcrowded ridge-top cemetery. What she feared most was a crowd of teenagers drawn by the useless death of one more young life wasted in a stupid, avoidable moment of carelessness, maybe without a seatbelt on, maybe showing off to kids in another vehicle. Three high school students from Rutledge had died just that way in two separate accidents in the last two months. One driver's little sister was sitting next to him in the front seat. Neither of them made it.

She was puzzled, too, about how she could possibly explain herself if anyone asked who she was or why she was there. She had never attended a funeral to which she didn't have to go. Her daughter told her once about a movie about a funeral crasher who went to funerals to pick up women because they were vulnerable there. Not likely here, she smiled. She probably would not see anyone she knew—she was still pretty far from home. Mostly, she did not want to do anything that might seem rude. She still cringed about the time she asked a woman at a picnic years earlier some question that caused the woman to ask her, "What are you doing? Writing a book about us?"

In any case, it was too late now. The police car ahead had barred the road again as the procession turned to the right onto a narrow road up a steep hill, only one lane wide though paved. A sign reading Piney Ridge Rd., hanging unevenly from a leaning post, had been used for target practice. The police car behind her turned off its blinking lights and started backing up to join the other police car, off-duty now.

She proceeded up the hill and around two steep curves. Then the cars ahead of her slowed, eventually stopping right in the middle of the road. She wasn't sure this was the final destination until she saw people getting out of their cars and pulling up their jacket hoods or opening umbrellas. She waited a decent interval and finally got out with the umbrella she always carried in the floor of the back seat. She walked up the road behind the crowd, noticing that every vehicle she passed seemed at least ten years old, about equally divided between pickups and sedans. A strong wind whipped the icy rain.

Ahead of her in the middle of the road an older man in a tan trench coat beckoned to her. "You're the last one," he said. "Come on so we can get started."

The crowd under a small awning numbered maybe twenty or so, many of them young adults but not teenagers. People, apparently family, sat in the one row of chairs in front. She stood back in the rain under her umbrella, not wanting to crowd in under the awning. On the far side of the awning she saw a plain rust-colored casket.

The man in the trench coat went around the right side of the awning and slowly walked down the front row shaking hands sadly with each person he passed. Two youngish men were seated on the right, then a slight woman with thinning gray hair pulled back in a bun, and next to her a young woman with a brown pony tail and two toddler-age children seated to her left.

About that time, a man standing nearby turned to the stranger and smiled. "Come on in out of the rain," he said. The uninvited guest was acutely conscious of her outsider status. Then she started wondering about the meaning of "guest." Do you get "invited" to a funeral? She had seen numerous engagement announcements in small country newspapers inviting "all friends and relatives" to the wedding, but never anything like that for a funeral. A death had to be certified by a public official; so, is a death a public event like a birth? One can't even leave a hospital with a newborn baby without registering the child with the appropriate public officials. And a marriage is a political matter too—has to be done in the name of the state. Lots of controversy about that these days.

Near the casket she noticed a tall figure standing in the rain, slightly hunched over against the wind with collar and hood pulled up tight. At first she couldn't tell if man or a woman. When the trench-coated man nodded slightly in that direction, the individual stepped forward under the awning and dropped her hood back. The guest thought she saw some sort of white collar, but it could have been just a shirt buttoned high against the weather.

* * *

Ellen Alsobrooks introduced herself to the assembled, said that the family had asked her to join with them today, and went on to welcome all of them to the sad and sacred occasion.

"Wayne's death is heartbreaking," she said, "Nothing any of us can say can take any of that heartbreak away. But we are called to gather together in hard times to seek what comfort we can from each other and from God. Part of our comfort will come from recalling all that was beautiful about Wayne Collier."

The guest, even from her remote point of view, saw the man at the right on the front row squirm in irritation.

Ellen continued. "For example, did you know Wayne loved birds? His family and friends say he was a real tough guy, so I guess he was. But his brother Dave told me that ever since Wayne was a little boy he had bird feeders outside his window and was always careful to keep them filled with seeds. Dave told me, too, that Wayne's favorite book was *The Sibley Guide to Birds* and that he owned two worn-out copies of it. He kept one by his bed and one in the truck.

"I want to tell you about something I saw yesterday on my way to meet this family. Remember that patch of sunlight we had for just half an hour yesterday afternoon? It had already rained two and a quarter inches by then, but for just a few minutes the clouds parted and the sun came out. On my way up to Rutledge I sensed a quick motion to my right and saw a bird taking off. It was bigger than a blue jay, smaller than a hawk. But the amazing thing about it was its colors. The sun was gleaming right through the prettiest slate blue wings and the brightest orange tail feathers I ever saw." Ellen paused.

"That bird took my breath away. I couldn't imagine where it came from or what it was. I don't know much about birds, so I had to ask a friend about it. He told me it was an American kestrel, the most colorful raptor in the world, the smallest member of the falcon family. Some people even train them to fly from their arms. The males have brilliant slate-blue wings and unusually long orange tail feathers that end with a black band marked by creamy-white spots like a string of pearls. The females are less colorful— as usual." A ripple of assent fluttered from the women.

Ellen continued. "Then I looked up more about them. Do you know these kestrels are common all over the Americas, from Alaska to the bottom of Argentina? So why had I never seen one? They're not even endangered."

Now the men in the small crowd shuffled a little. They didn't like game wardens coming around telling them what they could shoot and when they could shoot it.

Ellen Alsobrooks stood absolutely still, making eye contact with everyone in the crowd until they relaxed a little. Then she looked directly at Jessie Harris.

"But here is the amazing thing about them. These American kestrels are monogamous. They mate for life after a courtship that consists of three phases. First the males engage in a dazzling aerial display to get the female's attention. They show off! Then they offer the female a piece of food, maybe a cricket or a tiny vole, in mid-air. As large as they are, American kestrels can hover like hummingbirds. Apparently they evolved this capacity to make them better hunters, so they can track their prey close to the ground and swoop down at the best possible moment." (*Oh dear!* thought the guest. *Now she's talking evolution. Not smart.*)

"After all this, the pair flies off to search together for a home to share. In due course they both help feed and take care of their chicks."

The crowd grew palpably quiet. After a moment Ellen continued. "I didn't know Wayne and Jessie, but now that I've met Jessie I realize I've seen them before. I like to eat at Bud's Catfish place over on the river, and two or three times while there I noticed a young couple with two little children. They got my attention because they were clearly in love. You could tell it by how they laughed together and how every once in a while he would feed her a bit of his fish or a hushpuppy and then turn to feed one of the children. I remember being surprised that a couple of young people who already had children could still be so in love. It made me want to go over and ask them their secret."

"That couple was Wayne Collier and Jessie Harris."

"Wayne was beautiful. God didn't have to make him beautiful, any more than God had to create so much beauty in that American kestrel. But God did it anyway."

After a pause she said simply, "Praise God for the life of Wayne Collier. The world will be saved by beauty. Let us pray."

Colonus

a novella

I know it was hard, my children, but one word
makes all those difficulties disappear.
That word is love. (Sophocles, Oedipus at Colonus*)*

Time: The plague years

Will Evans walked slowly toward the student center along the brick-lined campus path, his worn tweed jacket hanging loosely over the parentheses of his shoulder blades. Avoiding the glittering chatter of his tenth-reunion cocktail party under the huge tent outside the theater, he circled around the other side of Bronson Hall, the fine old Victorian building where he had taken most of his English courses in college.

Will always loved to read, but his favorite course in college was the filmmaking class he discovered his sophomore year. That was when all his passions converged for the first time, rising like a sudden spring storm on the Gulf Coast where he grew up. His passion for filmmaking, unlike a spring storm, endured.

The timing had not been good for Will to come. Los Angeles to North Carolina is a long way, and Will was just beginning production of a new made-for-TV movie. But when the alumni staff called six months earlier to ask him to be on a panel for alternative professions for humanities graduates, he felt he couldn't say no. Only a year earlier he had received an Academy Award for best documentary feature, and his name sometimes appeared in campus publications; so, they managed to persuade him his presence would be a contribution to the humanities.

Will smiled at their last argument, remembering Mandy Dalgrin, the girl he dated his sophomore year. Mandy was terrific to look at and had brains, too. But it was she who had broken off the relationship, pointing to their mutually incompatible goals: she wanted to have fun and all he wanted to do was contribute to humanity.

Looking back, Will now found strange his own feelings; in fact, Mandy was right. Will attributed his social conscience to Exeter, which opened new worlds from which he never fully returned. During his junior year he went to Nairobi to an international student conference organized by the school's imaginative headmaster. In Africa Will saw pervasive poverty for the first time and also the power of community to change people's lives. An introvert by nature, he became fascinated by the European crew filming a documentary of the conference. For the first time he realized that a camera creates a perfect triangle connecting eye, mind, and heart.

After the trip to Nairobi he found a way to live for the summer in Senegal, determined to learn everything he could about African literature and history. For academic credit he wrote a long paper on the relationship between poetry and politics in the works of Leopard Senghor. He traveled home east via Cairo, Bombay, and Singapore, then spent the end of the summer before his senior year volunteering at a Quaker work camp in Philadelphia.

When Will headed back south for college, it was natural for him to sign up for the university's volunteer work project during spring break. Instead of going to Florida—or in the case of many of his acquaintances to the Bahamas, Cancun, or Steamboat Springs—he and a couple hundred other students chose to spend their spring break working in service projects in various local, national, and international sites. Most of the working groups consisted of ten or fifteen people, including a faculty member.

That was how he met Anne Edwards, the other reason he came back for the reunion.

From the moment he first saw her during their group's orientation, Anne confused him. She was a striking brunette in her thirties at the time, tall, slender, with sparkling hazel eyes and olive skin that tanned easily. When she was quiet or thinking, she could appear plain. But when she smiled or engaged in conversation, her presence filled a room. Her mind was keen, he could tell, and clearly she had a passion for fairness and general good humor.

But who was this woman? Why was she there? Although she was faculty, she was not the designated leader in this project. She was just there. When introduced to her at that first orientation meeting, he could only mumble his name and glance away.

Will's unease increased two weeks later when they arrived at their spring-break site, a spartan lodge in a camp sixty miles south of Wheeling, West Virginia. This would be their base for construction projects in the surrounding Appalachian hollows. She was a professor, chair of the Classics Department, but here she was in jeans, boots, and work shirt like the rest of them.

What, exactly, was her role supposed to be? Certainly she was not the leader of their group. The spring-break program was run entirely by students, and Darla and Jerry were the group's efficient student co-leaders. It was they who had asked Anne to participate as a faculty member for this site, but beyond that Will could not figure out how he should relate to her. No one else in the group, including Will, had known her previously except Rinny, who had been a student in her Greek drama class two years earlier. Was this woman supposed to be their professor or one of them? Will had seen enough of some of his mother's friends to pray she wouldn't try to fit in with the students by acting their age instead of her own.

The first night in West Virginia she solved at least the problem of what they should call her. "I'm Anne," she smiled. "But only till you sign up for one of my classes. Then I'm Professor Edwards." That was fine with everyone except Rinny, who could not make herself call her professor by her first name.

And it was not fine with Will, who already knew he would not call her anything. His confusion had turned to consternation when he discovered she was also was from Texas and had gone to college with a younger sister of his mother.

So why could he not keep his eyes off her whenever she left or entered a room? Why did he glance so often in her direction, discretely enough, he hoped, not to be noticed. What kind of quasi-Oedipus complex was this? Whatever it was, it was all wrong and he was going to solve it by keeping his distance.

He found out more about her only gradually as he overheard her talking easily with other students, wondering how they could be so comfortable with her. He learned that her husband had been killed in an auto accident three years earlier, just long enough that she could talk about him with a glow of gratitude rather than pain.

In prep school—he usually called it high school—Will had read enough Plato to know that people learn best from people they love and that they tend to fall in love with their teachers. In the library he once came across an article in the *New York Times* about the problem with sexual relationships between students and teachers. Such relationships are always wrong, the author wrote, for the same reason that sexual relationships between doctors and patients or employers and employees are always wrong—because of the imbalance of power.

But Plato was no help in this situation because Anne was not his teacher any more than she was his peer. She didn't fit into any framework he had ever experienced. There were no categories for this. Next year was his senior year and all his courses would be in his major department. *Just as well,* he told himself. *I'll get through this week and that will be that.*

The schedule for the week's work was divided into two parts. For the first two days the group built a basketball court for a camp for inner city kids. They spent that night in an unheated barn at the camp, laying out their bedrolls like fifteen camouflaged slugs in concentric curves around the fireplace.

The day's work brought another surprise about her. She was good with tools. She handled a power skill saw with ease, keeping up with a crew of four who were measuring and stacking the lumber for the low bleachers. He overheard her telling the others about growing up on a farm and how she enjoyed working with wood. She was good at hammering, too. He admired her quiet reply when Rinny asked her how to use a hammer. "It's all physics and geometry," she said.

The remainder of the week they worked in three teams of five doing carpentry repairs at the homes of different families. Will was glad not to be working with her, but each night back at the lodge the surprises continued. They were reading the same Pat Conroy novel, and they alone of the group kept extensive journals. He could tell she knew a lot, but also that she had the upper hand of her knowledge. She loved to make connections. Making connections, he overheard her say to Meredith, is what education and life are all about.

By the end of the week Anne had assumed a comfortable place in the group, except with Will and except in one other regard. The great divide was music. The students had come armed with a vast array of their favorites, most of which were unfamiliar to Anne. On the rare occasion when she recognized a tune or a group, two or three students always jumped on it, pointing out with gleeful sarcasm that yes, their parents liked that one too. It became a spirited group project to educate Anne about music, but she never quite caught up.

The tension broke on Wednesday night. Passing through the kitchen where Anne and two others were taking their turn cooking dinner, Will was wearing a T-shirt printed with the name of a film he had worked on as a production assistant the previous summer. Anne had seen the movie on TV and asked him about the shirt.

Will talked animatedly about the project. Each time Anne mentioned a favorite scene, he told a story about how it was filmed. She listened intently as he described details of the production and anecdotes about the actors offstage, including the starring actress who also produced it.

For the first time Will felt comfortable with this woman, leading her into a world she knew nothing about. They talked about how they loved *Lonesome Dove*, both the book and the movie. He told her about a mini-series he had worked on about General Custer, and they laughed together at his account of the perils of riding bareback returning from the set one afternoon. He urged her to read the book from which the series was made. She promised she would.

Then, as suddenly as it arose, the subtle ease between them subsided and the insistent silence returned.

On the final evening of the week the group talked about families and siblings and ideal companions. When they asked Anne about her ideal mate, she spoke affectionately of her husband and the happy, easy years they had spent together. When they asked what her criteria for this relationship had been, she paused and said seriously, "There were three, probably the same three everybody has." The room hushed. "Sex, sex, sex." she said.

Anne had been so dignified all week, at first no one believed she actually said it. Then laughter rocked the room. Anne blushed, but everyone loved it—most of all Will, who laughed with a great, uninhibited laugh that rose straight from his depths.

It was time to leave. Anne was in the first car to pack up for the long drive back to campus. When she came to the barn to say goodbye to the group still working there, she gave everyone a warm hug. Turning last to Will, she stopped for a moment. "You have a gift," she said quietly. "What?" he asked, off-guard. "You have a gift," she repeated. Then she was gone.

All that had happened eleven years before. He had seen her rarely during his senior year, usually at a distance, and never at all since graduation. Once, shortly after their return from West Virginia, she invited the whole group to her house for dinner. He felt even more uneasy around her then, surrounded by so much evidence of her rich and varied life.

Will looked up from his memories to see Anne strolling in his direction from the student center, headed toward her office in Mercer Hall. She seemed just the same as she broke into a warm smile. They exchanged greetings and asked about each other's work. Anne said she had kept up with his career and was delighted about the Academy Award. "Was it heavy?" she asked. "Heavier than you would think," he replied. He told her he had just finished reading her most recent book.

Both seemed about to ask or say something else when the silence fell once again. Erasing a shade of hesitation on her face, Anne said she hoped to see him again sometime, shook hands, wished him well, and smiled as she turned back toward her office.

Will watched her walk away. Over the years he had come to see the spring-break project as something like a play: auditions, rehearsal, the excitement and anxiety of opening night, intense sympathetic magic among the cast, the illusion that somehow it would all last forever. Then the final curtain fell, the set was struck, and everyone went separate ways.

If he called Anne's name now, he would be walking straight into life with all its uncertainties, not into a script with a conclusion already written.

Then he remembered Anne's answer when Darla asked her what quality she thought made men most attractive. "Confidence," she replied.

Will Evans laughed out loud—the same vast, joyful laugh he laughed one memorable spring night an eternity ago, sixty miles south of Wheeling, West Virginia.

"Anne," he called out to her, "Anne!"

* * *

Sitting at his desk in the small office he used when he was not on location, Will watched the sienna dusk settle over downtown Los Angeles. The letter he had carried in his pocket for almost a week lay open on the desk in front of him, asking him to direct a joint Greek-Turkish production of a Greek play in the ancient theater at Ephesus in Turkey. From the time he opened it he knew he would say yes.

It made no sense to accept this assignment. Financially, even with careful planning, the budget would barely cover costs. Casting the production would be a mare's nest. Culture clashes would be inevitable, especially with the politics and history involved. The logistics of shooting inside a historic site eight thousand miles from home were staggering.

Will was anxious about the project to the point of fear. He was also elated.

Will Evans's success as a filmmaker had been almost unprecedented for someone so young. What others would attribute to talent and hard work, he ascribed to luck. Six years earlier he had been one of the only two candidates out of over a hundred applicants to be admitted to the UCLA directing program, apparently on the basis of the Greek plays he directed in college.

That was after his disastrous seven-month spin through Duke Law School. He hated law school. One day in the spring semester, during a break from Uniform Commercial Code, he walked into the registrar's office and quit.

After UCLA he worked two years for the Disney Channel, learning everything he could about the commercial side of the business. But filmmaking was his first love, and by then he could afford to start making documentaries. At the age of twenty-eight he won an Oscar for best documentary feature.

It was a piece he had done on how the lives of three Mexican families with members on both sides of the Rio Grande were affected by the environmental provisions of NAFTA and the impact of new economic patterns on their traditional family structures. What could have been a dull polemic became as inevitable as a Greek drama as the film unfolded a series of casual, even accidental, decisions and events that led to irretrievable tragedy.

But what made the film shine was the way Will gave all the participants in it the courage to speak their truth to the camera and often, for the first time, to each other. Will was bi-lingual in Spanish—his Aunt Mamie had seen to that early on—and he had the rare gift of eliciting the faith of strangers, both in him and in themselves.

Will picked up the phone and dialed. "Tsinakis here," answered a cultured voice in the measured tones of a language learned in adulthood.

Socrates Tsinakis had moved from Greece to San Francisco at the age of fifty-nine to live near his three sons and daughters-in-law. He never expected to leave Athens, where he had been a successful lawyer and been active in many civic enterprises, including the National Museum and the annual Drama Festival held in the Theater of Herodes Atticus on the slope of the Acropolis. In his early fifties, however, he had taken up in earnest the poetry writing and painting that he had loved since childhood.

After the death of his wife, Xenia, he began to conceive of a new life for himself in the most beautiful city in North America. He leased an apartment in Colonaki in Athens to maintain his claim on his native land, then gathered himself up for his long odyssey west.

Although he had imagined a quiet retirement for himself, Tsinakis almost immediately became a key figure in the well-organized and highly successful Greek-American community in California. To his surprise, his passion for politics survived the trans-Atlantic move, and he worked tirelessly for the election of Art Agnos as mayor of San Francisco. After that, except for his enthusiastic support of every Democratic presidential ticket, he concentrated primarily on his cultural interests, which resulted in the letter he wrote to the brilliant young director and filmmaker in Los Angeles a little over two weeks previous to Will's call.

"Yes," said Will Evans after a brief exchange of pleasantries. "I will do it. But I have some questions. May I ask you the ones I'm most curious about?"

"You may ask them all," said Tsinakis courteously. "But perhaps we might talk together in person. Could you come up on the shuttle on Friday? There are some people here who wish to meet you. If you can come, I will arrange a small dinner gathering. There we might have the opportunity to respond fully to your questions."

"Certainly," Will said. "I can leave on the 2:10 flight."

"Excellent. I will arrange for you to be met at the airport," said Tsinakis. "Will you be bringing your associate?"

"No," said Will, a little too quickly. "I will come alone."

"*Entaxi*, then. Fine. I will be happy when I see you tomorrow."

Will held the phone in his hand for a few moments with the receiver button depressed before dialing the next number. He felt as if he had been through this a hundred times before.

A woman's voice answered warily, "Hello?"

"Vicky, this is Will. Can you meet me for dinner at the Mandarin Empress? We need to talk."

"I'm sure I don't know why. I've told you what I'm going to do, and I'm tired, and I don't want to hear anything you have to say. Besides, I now prefer to be called Victoria."

"I have a new assignment. I'm going to Turkey for a shoot in April."

A long silence followed. Three months had passed since Will Evans and Victoria Meade had planned to be married on April 15.

They had lived together off and on since meeting while Will was at UCLA. Victoria was not in the theater program, but she frequently signed on for stage crews and set designs. She was ambitious in an unfocused way, and Will had been attracted to her both because she was a striking, long-legged blonde and because she was from the South. Unlike many Southern women, however, she had a certain individualism and flair, almost but not quite to the point of eccentricity. For one thing, she wore hats. She was bright enough and sometimes lively, and for a while it had seemed that their mutual interests would support a permanent commitment.

When Will left Disney to go on his own, he and Vicky formed a professional partnership. For a while they worked together satisfactorily on several projects, including the one that earned the Oscar.

"I'll meet you in forty-five minutes," she said peevishly.

After he hung up, Will spent some time going over his account books and wrote out a check. Then he glanced at his watch. The third call could wait until morning. There was a three-hour time difference between Los Angeles and Durham, and he could call Anne Edwards at her office tomorrow before he left on the shuttle for San Francisco. Right now, he only wanted to get over the immediate hurdle.

He folded the letter from Socrates Tsinakis and returned it to his breast pocket. The city below was now alive with lights, but Will barely noticed as he stood up, turned out the desk lamp, and headed down the back stairs to the street. He decided to walk up to the restaurant near Vicky's apartment, then come back later for his Bronco.

By the time they were halfway through the sweet-and-sour soup, Victoria was fully launched into her familiar litany.

"I sacrificed my career to help you with yours," she said shrilly, forgetting the low voice she sometimes practiced before a mirror. "I could have gotten into the UCLA program, too. I had good connections there. But I gave up everything to help you. Then you broke off our engagement, and now you're going off again to Timbuktu, and it's all your fault."

What Vicky really wanted was to be an actress. She had a few parts in junior college productions and in community theater before she moved at the age of twenty-nine from Pine Bluff, Arkansas, to Los Angeles, where she was sure she would be discovered at last. Instead, she happened onto Will Evans, a loner who longed for good company. She set out to get him. At the beginning he was not unwilling. Now she was panicking, because until tonight she had nursed the notion that she could get him back.

"We worked out the budget for the production business together, Vicky . . . Victoria. Your salary was higher than mine. You know that."

"But now you have all that money from the trust your parents set up for you. You owe me severance pay. I've got to be able to pay for my new acting classes."

This was not Victoria Meade's first plan for remaking her life. Earlier she had enrolled for brief periods in classes in television photography and set design. For a while she free-lanced as a location coordinator. Sometimes she talked of going into real estate.

Through all of this, Will felt honor-bound to help her meet her dreams. The moment came, however, when he realized that all Victoria ever dreamed of was dreams. She had fancies, but no focus.

Will was through, but he knew he would try one last time to be helpful. It was partly guilt. He wasn't quite sure why he still felt responsible, but now his certainty that their relationship was over braced him.

He smiled faintly.

"I called the Actor's Studio today and arranged to prepay the two-year course. That's what you wanted, isn't it?"

Victoria blinked in surprise. Even she had not expected this much. She quickly caught herself and continued what Will had come to call The Monologue.

"A lot of good it will do me. I'm too old now to make it in the movies. I should have taken those classes when I first came to L.A. I wish I had never had met you. Besides, there is the lease on the new apartment. I will need at least a year of rent to start my life over."

"This should take care of it," Will said as he handed her an envelope containing the check he had written.

"I'm going home now," said Will as he stood to pay the bill. Victoria Meade, for the second time of the evening, was speechless. Will walked out the double glass doors of the Mandarin Empress. He did not look back.

He slept that night better than he had in months.

The next morning Will called his landlord, Jack Cooke, who lived across the well-manicured lawn beyond the large pool. Will rented the gardener's house in this north Los Angeles estate, enjoying the quiet it afforded and the veneered quaintness of the pseudo-Tudor style.

"Jack, I will be in and out for the next few weeks, finishing some odds and ends and starting up a new project. It looks like I'll be in Turkey on location for the entire month of April next spring. I wanted you to know. Is there anything I can do to help you while I'm here?"

Jack Cooke had lived alone in the huge house since his wife died over a year earlier. Jack had pioneered serious made-for-television films, and for a while he headed the production of docudramas for CBS. He enjoyed Will's company and liked the young man's imagination and grit. When Will's schedule allowed, the two men enjoyed sitting around the pool with a bottle of scotch and lots of good talk. "I just made some pancakes, Will. Come on over and join me. I'll be out with a hot stack for you in a couple of minutes."

"Okay, but not for long. I'm going up to San Francisco today for a meeting about the new project. I'd like to talk with you about it."

As Will eased his long legs under the round table by the pool, he felt the same comfort and curious anticipation he experienced the first time he met Jack Cooke. He had never known anyone quite like this older man—crusty, smart, surprisingly tender for someone who had been in the business so long.

Even though he had no children, Jack never treated Will like a son. He had too much regard for his separateness for that. It was rather as if Will were a younger colleague, a kind of co-conspirator or collaborator, maybe someone who would continue what he himself had tried to begin.

The two men also shared a quiet, crenelated sense of humor, laughing sometimes happily and long with an ease rare for both of them. Without ever saying so, each recognized that the other was reaching for something outside the ordinary.

"Okay, Will, what is it?" Jack asked as he arranged the plates on the table and handed Will a small silver pitcher of warmed maple syrup.

"I've been asked to film a production of a Greek tragedy at an ancient theater in Turkey. It's the damnedest thing. A group of Greek-Americans in San Francisco got together with some Turkish businessmen to apply for a grant for a joint project. They got the grant, and they want me to direct it. The only problem is, there's no way it will work."

"Why not?"

"Oh, come on, Jack. Greeks and Turks have been killing each other for four hundred years. Or rather, Turks have been killing Greeks, depending on who you're talking to. That's before we even start talking about getting together an international cast and crew for this thing and then keeping them together. Or filming live in an ancient outdoor theater in Turkey, of all places."

"Is it the theater at Ephesus?"

"Yes. Have you been there?"

"Once, thirty years ago. It is one of the most beautiful places I have ever seen. Seats 25,000 people. Brother Paul wrote about it in Acts 19. You should look it up. Why did they choose you?"

"I don't know. I guess I'll find out later today. I'll be meeting with some of them when I go up to see Socrates Tsinakis."

"Tsinakis? I met him here at a fundraiser during the last campaign. He's an unusual guy. Quiet. Civil. A powerful presence in any public gathering, but there's something private about him, too, like he knows a good bit more than he's saying. He looks at you with a gaze that could pass right through one of those Greek icons he collects."

"Jack, I'm not sure I'm up to this. I may be in over my head."

"Take your time. Break it down into pieces. Then put the pieces together again like a mosaic. But you know all of that already. Unless, of course, you don't want to do it at all."

"I want to do it very much."

"Seems to me that everything you've ever done has prepared you for this. You've already worked in foreign locations. You don't know Greek or Turkish, but you're bi-lingual in Spanish, and once you know any other language fluently, you know the world's organized in more than one way. Besides, didn't you direct some Greek plays in college?"

"There were three of them. The first I did in a small workshop to get out of writing a paper for a Greek civilization course. But the idea caught on, and the Classics Department sponsored a production both my junior and senior years. We rehearsed in the late spring, then presented the plays at the outdoor theater on the campus during the last three weekends in May. School kids came from all over and lots of community people, too. I did Sophocles' *Antigone* and *Oedipus Rex*, then got daring and put on Aristophanes' *Lysistrata* after I graduated and no one could expel me."

"What will you be doing in Turkey?"

"Sophocles' last play, *Oedipus at Colonus*. He wrote it when he was ninety."

Jack smiled at the thought. "I don't know it."

"It's the best of all. It's the one that changes everything."

Will gave Jack a brief summary of the play as he finished another plate of pancakes.

"Well, you're right. You're going to need some help. You better take the best assistant director you can find."

"What about you?" Will asked, half joking to hide his hope.

"Hell, I'm not old enough. A dozen years to go before I make it to Sophocles' age. Anyway, I'm not traveling much these days. Better try Gil Manning. But I'll be right here anytime you want to talk about it."

"Thanks, Jack. I'll count on that." As he rose to go, Will paused. "By the way, things are over with Vicky."

Jack Cooke smiled, barely masking his pleasure at this news. After pausing a moment for the sake of courtesy, he said: "*Al enemigo que huye, un puente de plata.*"

"She got that, too," Will smiled wanly.

Will planned his return from San Francisco to L.A. on Saturday afternoon in time to get by for his weekly visit with his friend Emile Ardolino, whom he had first met when Ardolino gave a guest lecture in the UCLA theater program.

By that time Ardolino had already won an Oscar for his documentary *He Makes Me Feel Like Dancin'*, then made a breakthrough to the big screen with *Dirty Dancing* and *Sister Act*. Even though he was already very sick, he recently had been able to finish directing *The Nutcracker*.

Like most gay men, Emile hated hospitals and was determined to die at home. For four months Will had been going to see him every Saturday at 5:00 P.M. If he was out of town, he never failed to call at five in the afternoon. In earlier weeks when

Emile had been up to it, Will would take him out for a drive or on an errand.

Emile appreciated deeply that Will scheduled his visits out of his care for him rather than his own convenience. Emile had been a little dubious at first—a Texan filmmaker sounded like an oxymoron. But quickly he came to admire the young man's vision and feel for his work as well as his capacity for friendship.

Will also possessed the gift—Emile with his director's sensibility knew how rare a gift it is—of being able to keep silent in a way that rests easy in a room.

"How do you feel today?" Will asked simply. He meant it. Emile knew it is possible to tell in an instant whether the person asking that question wants an answer or not. Most don't.

"It's been a quiet day. Not too much pain. How was San Francisco?"

"Emile, I need some advice."

Tears of gratitude welled up in Emile's eyes. He was bone weary of being a patient. He was a *director*, by God, and would be till the day he died if dementia didn't get him first. AIDS had not robbed him of what he knew how to do.

Will talked about the project, his concerns about casting and assembling the crew and working in Turkey and the political hazards and bringing the whole thing together.

After a while Emile said, "You are going to need the best assistant director you can find. You should try Gil Manning."

"You're the second person this week to tell me that."

"You're the boss, but he will be the linchpin, the one who makes it work. Sorry, Will, but if you're working in Turkey it's got to be a he. If you do your job right, you will be responsible for everything but you've got to maintain a light touch. He will be your technical guy and also your eyes and ears. And he'll be the heavy when you need one. You'll need one.

211

"But get everybody else, especially the leads, lined up first. If the chemistry is wrong, it will bollix everything. Believe me, that is something I learned the hard way."

Will sensed that Emile was growing tired. Rising to leave, he leaned over and gave his friend a big hug.

That was another thing Emile loved about Will. How many straight friends did he have who were so secure they could hug a gay guy? Hell, *love* a gay guy? With AIDS?

"See you later," said Will simply.

"So long." Emile replied. "Thanks for coming."

By tacit agreement they no longer said goodbye.

* * *

Anne Edwards sat midway back in the sweep of chairs reserved for faculty on the lawn in front of the Duke Chapel. The October morning greeted a campus transformed by streaming banners and glorious fall foliage for the inauguration of the new president. The faculty in their regalia looked like a flock of rare tropical birds, with a scattering of egrets and a large contingent of penguins, posing for photographs at a zoo.

Anne was sitting next to her friend and colleague Sofia Filonov. As a handsome woman entered the stage in the company of the white-haired chair of the Board of Trustees to a roar of applause, the two professors glanced at each other with a wry smile. An acute observer might have noticed a trace of irony behind their smiles. Neither Anne Edwards nor Sofia Filonov could have said this was the moment they had been working toward their entire careers at Duke University, because neither of them imagined that the University in their lifetime would inaugurate a woman as president.

The two friends had joined the Duke faculty immediately after graduate school at a time of so much expansion in American universities that there were jobs even for women. Most of their colleagues assumed they were "affirmative hires," but Anne and Sofia knew better. That came later, and even after affirmative action became a stated goal of many universities, it occurred far more rarely than most male faculty assumed. Many men preferred to conclude that any woman who was hired got the job because she was female, not because she was good.

Anne turned her attention back to the new president, who was saying at that moment: "In closing I propose three definitions. First, to be educated persons in our society means to know our place in history. Second, to be a purposeful person means to choose what to do about it. Finally, to be a happy person means to feel gratitude for those who went before and responsibility to those coming later."

She continued: "On this happy occasion, it would be ungrateful for me to assume that I come into this position solely on my own merits. I would not be here at all if it were not for the many people who came before me, including the brave women in higher education generally and at this institution in particular. I thank them, and I thank the trustees, faculty, and every one of you here for this new era of opportunity for us all."

Then, with a wide smile the new president concluded: "And one more thing: If we do this right, we'll have some fun."

Anne and Sofia stood applauding joyfully with all the others, knowing that this occasion marked the unspoken moment when a tide stands still before turning to flow in the other direction.

As Anne turned to leave, she instinctively scanned the ranks of faculty sitting in front of her. At that moment, Hal Askew turned to look back at her, a big grin lighting his face, his right fist raised to half-mast in an old sixties salute. Anne beamed back, inclining her head slightly in knowing complicity.

213

As usual when Anne saw Hal, her heart quickened. Harold Askew was a brilliant history professor, a born scholar who never lost touch with the ways of the Nebraska cornfields where he grew up. Hal and Anne had been a little in love with each other for years and likely always would be. If Hal were anywhere in her presence, even in a large lecture hall, Anne always knew he was there. It was as if there were an invisible dance between them, choreographed by mutual interests, attraction, and friendship. After Wes's death, it seemed for a while that a decision might arise between them. Anne made sure, however, that they never veered close enough to those shoals for the question to be raised. Hal was married to a woman Anne knew slightly and admired, and one of Anne's few unbendable feminist scruples was that a woman never tries to take another woman's man. In time, Hal found tactful ways to shade his relief with appropriate protests of dismay, and the two continued to confine their relationship to an occasional lunch or animated greeting on campus.

Anne Edwards was on academic leave for the entire year. She decided to drop by her office in Mercer Hall before going to the reception for the new president.

Anne's friend and assistant Laura Corlew rose to meet her as she entered the office. "How was it?" she asked.

"Glorious," replied Anne. "I didn't expect to live to see the day."

Laura was bright and curious, and ordinarily she would have asked for details of the inaugural speech.

Now she said worriedly, "Anne, there are two messages for you. Your father called from Santa Fe. And someone named Will Evans called from Los Angeles. Both asked that you call back. Your father's at home. Will said he would be leaving for a plane about an hour from now, Pacific Time."

A ghost of a smile passed across Anne's face before her expression clouded. "Do you have any idea what Dad is calling about? How did he sound?"

"I couldn't tell," said Laura guardedly. "But he didn't say it wasn't urgent." Anne went into her office and closed the door.

She sat down, took a deep breath, and dialed the 505 area code followed by the number of her father's home on Tano Ridge Road in Santa Fe. He answered on the second ring.

"Clay Edwards," he said simply.

"Hello, Dad. Laura said you called. I just came in from the inauguration of the new president. She is wonderful. But what's going on? Are you okay?"

Her father paused for a moment, then said, "Richard went into a coma last night." In a low voice thick with pain he added, "I think we're going to lose him."

"Oh, no. He had been doing so well."

"That's what the doctors thought, too, but they're worried. Ian Trevor-Smith was just here. He'll be back later this afternoon. I wanted you to know."

"Can they tell what happened?"

"Not exactly. It may have been a stroke. Maybe something crossed over into his brain. He's struggling to breathe."

Richard Dellavecchia was the executive director of the Santa Fe Opera. A brilliant musician trained as a tenor at Julliard, he had moved to Santa Fe because of the opera and had sung leading roles in *Traviata*, *La Bohemé*, *Andrea Chenier*. The last was his favorite. As the condemned prisoner ascends the ramp to the guillotine, Richard always felt a powerful infusion of confidence in the ultimate worth of his own life.

After HIV took over and his energy began to flag, Richard moved over into management and served as production manager before the board of directors named him executive director two years previous. The successful season ended in August, and Richard's health began to decline.

Anne thought of Richard as a beloved brother. They enjoyed cooking together during her visits to Santa Fe, and, in front of the kiva fireplace, they carried on long conversations about books, movies, and writing. Especially about writing. Richard had published two short stories and was at work on a novel.

"Have you called Serena?"

"Not yet. I wanted to talk with you first. She was here just last week."

"Dad, I'm coming to Santa Fe. There's an American flight from Raleigh-Durham through Chicago at 4:38 this afternoon. It arrives in Albuquerque around 8:30. I'll catch the 9 o'clock Shuttlejack."

"Anne, I'm not going to tell you not to come. I really would appreciate it. I can meet you at the Inn at the Loretto at 10:15." After a pause he added, "Thank you."

"You're welcome," Anne said. "And Dad, hang in there."

"I'll try, Hon."

Anne Edwards called the American Advantage number to arrange her flight, leaving the return open. Then she glanced at the clock she kept on the wall opposite her desk. She still had time to go by home, pack a few things, and get to the airport by 4:00.

As she stood to leave, she remembered the other message. Maybe she could still catch Will Evans in Los Angeles.

Anne had no idea what this was about.

"Hello, Will? This is Anne Edwards in Durham. I understand you called. It's good to hear from you. How are you?"

"I'm fine, thanks. I hope you are. Do you have a minute?"

"Sure."

"Anne, something has come up that I would like your help with if you can possibly find time. A group in San Francisco has received grants from the Arts and Humanities Endowments to produce a film version of one of Sophocles' plays for PBS and maybe for a feature release, too. They've asked me to direct it, and I've said yes. I'm leaving in a few minutes to fly up to San Francisco to talk with the sponsors. We're going to produce and film it in the theater at Ephesus."

"That's wonderful news. You'll do great."

"I haven't done a Greek play since college, and I'm nervous. I was hoping we could arrange a time for me to tell you more about the project. There's a piece of it I hope you can help with."

Anne looked again at the clock. "Will, I'll be happy to call you back later, but I'm catching a plane in a little while to visit my father in Santa Fe. Can this wait?"

"How long will you be in New Mexico?"

"I don't know. Dad's not in good health, and I want to spend some time with him."

"I need to go to New York to take care of something for the production. If it's not an imposition, I could fly through Albuquerque and come up to Santa Fe for the day. Could you get away for lunch?"

Anne smiled at the receiver. This was not the diffident undergraduate she remembered. "Yes, all right. That would be fine. I'll give you Dad's number in Santa Fe. Call me when you know your plans, and if I'm still there, we can get together."

As Will wrote down the number, he asked, "Where is your favorite place to eat?"

"Well, you know us Texans. It has to be Mexican. I like Maria's."

"Maria's it will be. I'll call you in Santa Fe on Tuesday. I hope everything goes well in the meantime. Thank you, Anne."

"Thanks, Will. I'm glad you called. *Hasta la vista*."

Anne parked her blue Volvo by the curb so she could walk up the long sidewalk through the leaves to the porch of her Dutch Colonial house. The leaves on the tulip poplars on either side of the walk were floating down like the handkerchiefs of Victorian flirts. Anne took a moment to notice her pleasure at scuffling through them. They were brittle enough to sound like the mother skunk with her four kits she once saw on a country road, skittering slantwise across the pavement like a tiny British regiment.

How dare the day be so beautiful? Anne grimaced, instantly appalled at her ingratitude.

When she entered the house, she went straight to the telephone cubby off the kitchen to call her sister Serena in Chicago. Serena's housekeeper reported that she had gone to her board meeting. Anne knew the number by heart.

"Planned Parenthood," answered the receptionist.

"This is Serena McCauley's sister Anne Edwards calling. Is Serena available?"

"Her board meeting is just finishing, Ms. Edwards. I'll see if I can get her."

In a moment Serena came on the line.

"Hi, Serena. Dad called today about Richard. He's gone into a coma, and I'm flying out to Santa Fe on the 4:38 flight this afternoon. I have a layover in Chicago at 5:45 for almost an hour. Can I call you when I get there?"

"Better yet," said Serena, "I'll come out to meet you. But tell me what's going on."

They talked briefly, Anne telling her what little she knew. Serena was less surprised than Anne.

"I was there last week on my way home from the national meeting in Los Angeles. It was clear that Richard is going down fast. I'm heartsick to hear. Should I come with you?"

"Serena, let me go first. I'll call if we need you. Besides, you have a lot going on. Doesn't Camille's ballet open this weekend? How is she doing?"

Camille was Anne's favorite niece. One of the nice things about nieces and nephews is that you can get by with having favorites. At fourteen, Camille had an unusual self-confidence almost completely attributable to ballet. Camille's concentration on making her body do its work deflected her preoccupation with the usual teenage struggles, although she still spent longer hours in front of a mirror than she wanted anyone to know. Camille reminded Anne of Serena at the same age—kind and good, entirely unselfish and without pretense.

"She's doing beautifully. I've seen the dress rehearsal, and it's lovely. Anyway, the most important thing right now is what's going on in Santa Fe. I can come immediately if you think I should. In the meantime, I'll see you later this afternoon at O'Hare."

"The traffic will be horrific. Let me just call you."

"I'll be at your gate," Serena said simply. "What is your flight number?"

* * *

Anne backed her father's tan Explorer out of the garage, turned it around carefully in the landscaped drive, and pulled slowly out onto Tano Ridge Road. The drive down into Santa Fe never failed to delight her. At night the city lay like a low coffer of shining jewels. By day it looked like a monochrome outcropping of earth-colored mounds containing hidden treasures, guarded magisterially by the purple Sandia Mountains rising beyond. Even the fierce traffic wheeling down from Taos never diminished her delight.

Anne's pleasure today was heightened by feelings she could not quite identify, a mix of curiosity and anticipation. Shaking her head slightly to clear her thoughts, she determined to admit only the curiosity.

She drove straight down St. Francis toward the busy intersection at Cordoba. After a left turn she pulled immediately into the parking lot behind Maria's.

This was a moment Anne had never learned to approach without foreboding. She dreaded the thought of having to wait, maybe in vain, for a man she was supposed to meet. She hated to appear pitiful. Once she had been stood up at an academic conference by an attractive but untrustworthy colleague at another university who had invited her to meet him for a drink at the bar at ten, but did not show up. The next day he said breezily he had been watching the latest episode of *Dallas* and just forgot.

Will was standing in the outer entrance hall, reading a copy of the free local newspaper stacked on a stand by the door. When Anne entered, he smiled broadly, touched her shoulder in a gesture of greeting, and said "Hello. Thanks for coming."

Anne smiled back. "Hi. It's good to see you."

Will guided her down the hall and through the larger dining room into the small room where a fire was blazing in the kiva fireplace. He could not have known that this was her favorite room in the restaurant. The cantina bar through the opposite door was charming with its colorful frescos, bartered half a century earlier by a local artist in exchange for food and drink from Maria, but this cozy room a step or two down from the others always felt to Anne like a sanctuary.

On the table closest to the fireplace was a glass vase of irises, mauve and yellow. Anne had seen them somewhere before. In a painting.

"'What I need most are flowers, always flowers,'" she murmured.

"Monet," Will said.

Their eyes locked in mutual recognition. After a moment, they both glanced away in confusion. How did he know that? she wondered.

"I brought them for you," Will said.

"Thank you," said Anne. "They're lovely."

Two glasses were already in place along with salsa and chips. "I ordered margaritas for us," he said as he seated her facing the fire. "I hope that's all right."

"Perfect," said Anne. "Thank you."

As they raised their glasses, Anne permitted herself a second look at Will, trying to identify what was different about him.

At twenty Will Evans had been heart-stoppingly beautiful—over six feet tall by two or three inches, skin the color of nutmeg, medium brown hair, improbable turquoise eyes, with reverse curves around his lower lip like a Henry Moore sculpture.

She recalled how startled she had been when she put it together that she had seen Will long before she ever met him. It was in the museum in Delphi, the Bronze Charioteer. When Melina Mercuri was finally able to return to her beloved Greece after the colonels' tyranny, she made a documentary of her favorite sites. Toward the end she said, "Now, Ah weel show you the mahn Ah lawve. Ah *lawve* heem." The young man standing there alone, in perfect poise while holding the reins of four horses, heels together but bare left foot slightly turned to the side for balance. His hair held in a leather band tooled with a Greek key design, tied casually at the back. But it was the mouth—that was it—below his straight nose, full upper and lower lips quietly together.

Years before, Anne had been alone in that room with the Charioteer. It was an early morning before the droves of tourists arrived; even the guard left briefly to smoke a cigarette. Suddenly the sun splayed through the high window over the Charioteer's head. It was as if Will had been the model for this statue. Anne suspected that Will had learned early and unconsciously to deflect attention from himself by adopting a slightly askance demeanor. His hair was usually a little awry.

"To our noble selves," smiled Will.

"Yes," Anne echoed, "to our noble selves."

"Mamie's toast," Will continued. "Always the same."

"I want to know who this Mamie is with her wonderful toast," Anne said. "But first of all, catch me up on yourself. We didn't talk much at your reunion. How have you been?"

"When I went to Los Angeles, it was a huge leap into a very uncertain future. The directing program at UCLA was excellent, and after that I was really lucky to get the job at Disney. It was a great apprenticeship."

He hesitated. "Then came that horrible day in Dallas." Will gazed again into the fire.

"What are you talking about?" Anne asked fearfully. She had never fully recovered from that horrible day in Dallas on November 22, 1963. No one of her generation ever would.

"Do you remember that Delta flight that crashed in a wind shear during a rainstorm at DFW?"

"Yes," Anne said, dread rising. Will paused again.

"My parents were both on it."

"Oh, my God!" Anne exclaimed.

Over the years Anne had learned the hard language of sympathy, hard because it had to be pruned as spare as a branch in a Japanese print.

After a moment she said quietly, "I'm so sorry."

Anne's calm encouraged Will to continue.

"They were coming back from Europe. They were never very happy with me after I chose Los Angeles. I'm not sure they were ever very happy with me, period. From the time I was a small child, I remember their saying that they never wanted any more children after me. I was closer to my father in some ways than my mother, but he was furious when I decided to make films for a living. He took me to see the Astros in the Astrodome when I was a child. I never could figure out why he always wore a suit to the games."

Anne listened intently, knowing the gyres in which grief causes mourners to wander.

She already knew Will was an only child. During his work on *Antigone* for his senior thesis, she had told the cast that one of the most important things to know about people was whether they had siblings and how they felt about them. Sophocles' play, she told them, was about brothers and sisters, Ismene and Antigone as much as Eteocles and Polyneices. Will had told her that his lack of experience in this matter made it harder for him to direct the play.

"How did you cope?"

"Same way I always did. Mamie."

"Mamie?"

"She is my father's older sister, twelve years older. His only sibling. From the age of five I spent most of my summers with her on her ranch near Gonzales. Mamie is one tough cookie. Once when I was playing in a mound of dirt near a cattle tank, a five-foot rattlesnake crawled near my feet and was headed into a hole just as Mamie walked up. She grabbed the snake by the tail, yanked it out of the hole, and beat it to death against a rock.

"This is the same woman who can rope a calf, dress like a fashion plate when she wants to, string a barbed-wire fence, and hire interior decorators from Dallas—she never did like Houston, although it's closer—to redo the ranch house, much to the horror of her neighbors. She is fond of saying that the ranch is twenty miles west of Gonzales, eighty miles east of Austin, and three hundred miles due south of Neiman-Marcus."

223

Anne smiled. She knew women like this. They were a breed peculiar to the Southwest, creatures of the nineteenth century even if they were born in the twentieth.

"Mamie made me speak Spanish with her from the start," Will continued. "She thought every Texan should, but with her it was more than that. 'Boy,' she would say to me, 'it's a big world out there. I want you to see as much of it as possible. But if you can speak another language, you can carry another whole world around in your head without ever leaving home.'"

"How did she become so different from your father?"

"Their mother read all the time. She was ambitious for her children, too. Somehow she got her firstborn out of Texas and all the way up East to college. Mamie went to Smith. She came home from New York to take over the ranch when my father decided he wanted to go into business in Houston.

"Mamie understood Dad better than he understood her. He just thought she was weird. I adore her. Mamie Kokernot never leaves a herd on a dark night."

"Kokernot?"

"After she came back to Texas she was married for a couple of years to a nearby rancher. The divorce was amicable, as they say. Lots of men came courting—still do, for that matter, even though she's sixty-seven years old—but she's not interested. She smiles, takes them for a ride around the ranch in her pick-up, feeds them a good meal, then sends them packing."

"How did your parents get along with each other?"

"Pretty well," Will said. "Just not with me. They didn't want to be bothered."

Anne remembered reading somewhere that Robert Louis Stevenson said the children of lovers are orphans.

"But I've been talking about myself far too much. I want to hear about you. Let's have a second margarita and I'll do the listening."

"A two-margarita lunch?" Anne laughed. "Sure. Why not?" Will signaled the server unobtrusively.

"Tell me about your family," he said.

Anne paused, not sure how much to say. Know your audience, she reminded herself before most classes she taught and every public speech she gave.

But who was this Will Evans anyway? How much do you say to someone like this? She took a deep breath. Okay, she said to herself. But easy now.

"I can start with my family of birth, or I can start with Wes. Which would you prefer?"

Anne didn't realize it was a test until she said it.

"Start at the beginning," Will said quietly, nodding encouragement.

"I have two older brothers. They've always fought with each other, and now they're fighting over what will happen to the family inheritance. And I have a younger sister. I'll start with Serena. We all have family names, but Serena is the best named because it fits her exactly. We are very different, don't even look alike. Serena has blue eyes and curly hair like our mother. She has one of the calmest temperaments I've ever seen. She was that way from birth. One of my earliest memories is standing over her crib watching her smile in her sleep. She told me recently that she took a stress assessment in a women's magazine and scored a one on a scale of one to ten. Everyone has always loved her. She's pretty amazing."

Remembering her own caution about details, not generalities, she continued. "I also learned early not to underestimate her. She had a pretty traditional Texas upraising. She

225

was a cheerleader in high school, made good grades, and always had lots of dates. She went to SMU, pledged Kappa, majored in early childhood education, and married an up-and-coming guy from East Texas. She has three children, whom I adore—especially her daughter Camille. Things changed for her pretty drastically before she moved to Chicago. But that's another story."

Anne paused. "Let's eat," she suggested. Will agreed, turning to the Carne Adovada in front of him, a traditional northern New Mexico dish he chose after reading the parenthesis in the menu: ("Critically acclaimed by Santa Fe natives as the best anywhere"). Anne had selected her favorite, her test of any Mexican restaurant: chile rellenos.

For a while they enjoyed the quiet, glancing instinctively from time to time toward the fire.

In time, Anne said, "But are we here to talk about family?"

"In a way, yes," responded Will. "I've agreed to direct one of Sophocles' plays next April in the ancient theater in Ephesus. It's funded by a combination of Greek- and Turkish-Americans, and both the national endowments are supporting the project. They cannot contribute to the filming in Turkey because it is outside the U.S., but they will underwrite the editing and preparation of the film for the Masterpiece Series on Public Television."

"Which play is it?" Anne asked.

"*Oedipus at Colonus.*"

"That's my favorite." Anne said.

"I know," Will said.

"My hope is that you might be willing to join us as a classics consultant on the film."

Anne raised her eyebrows. "Tell me more."

"We would need you there for three to four weeks. We'll pay your expenses, of course, and a modest honorarium. None of us knows the ancient plays like you do."

"I've never done anything like this before."

"Neither have I," Will smiled.

Anne looked down for a few moments, then raised her eyes. "I'll have to sleep on this. May I call you tomorrow?"

"Tell you what. The La Fonda Hotel is right here, and I've always wanted to stay there. Would you be free to meet me there for breakfast in the morning?"

This time Anne smiled: "I'll see you in the morning at the Plazuela at 9:00 A.M."

The next morning they arrived at the same time. They sat in a corner so they could talk quietly and still see the colorful decor in every direction.

Anne began. "First of all, of course, I talked with my father about it. As usual, he was immediately supportive of anything I choose to do. I don't know how I was so fortunate to land him as a father.

"His overwhelming concern right now is about his partner Richard. Between you and me, I'm afraid Richard might not make it much longer. But if the timing is right for Dad by next spring, and if he still feels well enough to travel and wants to go, I'd love to take him to Athens. He's always wanted to go there. Maybe Serena could come with us and stay with him while I'm in Turkey."

She added, "When Dad was president of the National Conference of Mayors, he met the mayor of Athens who invited him to visit anytime and stay with him at his place in Colonaki at the corner of Scoufa and Democritous streets.

"I've been thinking, too, about how hard it is to turn a stage play into a film. Maybe we could use five or six cameras. Of course, that would require a terrific film editor. I've been following the

227

career of Julie Block. She would be great. And there's a great old hotel, the Kalehan, just a stone's throw from the theater, that would accommodate the whole crew."

Anne smiled and paused. "But I'm getting ahead of myself. Yes, Will, I will do it. I would love to."

"Will, what was it that happened between us in Appalachia?"

"I don't know," Will said, as easily as if picking up the thread of a recent conversation. "I've thought about it for years. Some people talk about a kind of electro-magnetism, something about how ions line up. Others call it pheromones, whatever the hell they are. I think it was an instant, mutual recognition of each other's inner self."

Anne thought as she often did about words and the meaning of words. "The Greeks had a term for the inner self," she said. *Autos entos.* The self inside. We call it authenticity."

"Yes," said Will. "That's exactly right. For the first time in my life I felt recognized for who I am. I felt known. Not only known, but valued. Of course, it didn't hurt, either, that you were and are absolutely gorgeous. Beauty and brains—oh my!

"So naturally, for a while I started fantasizing that you and I might get married someday. That went on for about three years. Then I wondered if maybe we could become cherished friends for the duration. I know how improbable this all seems, given the distance of time and talk between us. But it did not go away. Still hasn't."

Anne, too, felt free to speak her own truth. "Will, I confess I too wondered many times about the possibility of our marrying. Oddly, my reservations did not lie in the age difference between us, or even the direction in which it goes. You and I are both independent people, and we will continue to grow whatever happens. And with so many shared passions, we would continue to grow together.

"I did worry more, of course, about the matter of children. Wes and I could not have any because he suffered a severe case of the mumps as a child. We wrestled hard with that, but in time we both became comfortable with our situation, and I learned to love the additional time it gave me to nurture our extended families, our communities, and my students. And of course, I do have Serena's three children, whom I adore, in my orbit.

"No, my reservations lay elsewhere. They have to do, first, with the times in which we each have lived. Our contexts are different. We have read many of the same books, of course, and liked many of the same movies. But the histories that have shaped us have been different. This may not be important to everyone, but it is to me. The world events that have shaped me are different from those that have informed you. It's almost as if our eyes have evolved with a different focus."

Will listened intently. "I hadn't thought of it that way. Now I begin to understand that part of our being out of focus with each other has to do with our very age difference. Because you are older, you know the events I have experienced—but I cannot know the times ahead of me that you have seen."

Then Will added: "This is all a little confusing, and I will have to think about it. You will too. But I know this for sure: I will be there for you for the rest of your life. You can count on it. I love you."

"I love you, too."

* * *

As a child, Will looked forward, all summer long, to going into Gonzales with Mamie for errands. From the time he was six his aunt let him drive her big white Chevrolet truck both ways on the three-mile dirt road between the house and the gate. By fourteen he was driving the whole way. Texas still let farm kids get an early driver's license, and Mamie saw to it among her friends at the Department of Public Safety that Will qualified.

On the Saturday morning trips to town, Mamie always went first to the post office, then to the tiny county library in the basement of the courthouse where each of them returned and checked out another armload of books. Will's favorite stop was the feed and seed, the meeting place for every serious farmer and the few weekend ranchers in Gonzales County. You could generally tell which ones were which by the size of their belt buckles. The real ranchers' belts were fixed with seviceably large buckles whereas the wannabees had trouble sitting down. This is where Mamie howdyed with her friends. If it happened to be raining that day and the men couldn't get into the fields, they'd hang around even longer. The manager, Bill Buckner, put in a pot-belly stove and some old benches in the back for that purpose. Those rainy days were the ones Will liked best. No one paid much attention to him. They knew who he was and took him for granted, which meant he overheard far more than they knew.

For one thing, Will noticed that Mamie's presence always affected the men in the store for the better. Their bawdy jokes and macho posturing faded when she came in the door. They stood up a little straighter, wiped a hand on a shirt. They didn't take off their caps—Texas men don't do that except, sometimes, inside for a meal—but some of the older ones would touch their brim in a gesture of respect, then pretend they meant to smooth back their hair. Mamie herself sometimes had a slightly off-color story or joke to tell, and soon they would all be laughing and carrying on.

Will thought all the men looked weathered, old, and wise. He assumed they were also all-powerful. It hurt his feelings real bad one day when he overheard this conversation:

I've got a hunnerd acres of hay down on the ground, and it's been wet for three days. May lose it.

But you knew it was goin' to rain. Why d'ya cut it?

My boss told me to.

Will hated to think of any of these men having bosses.

Will also watched with keen interest the few women who came in. One woman, thin and harried-looking, always came in alone, usually to pick up an order of supplies, with her three skinny, runny-nosed children. He didn't worry that the children were often barefoot—he went barefoot too all he could—but he worried about the woman. He knew she was married, never saw her husband, heard rumors about "demon rum." One day the woman had on sunglasses that didn't quite cover the purple patch around her eye. He wondered.

The feed and seed was the site of the rural-Texas town meeting, where the transactions tended to conclude in seemingly offhand conversations conducted in low tones: arrangements to swap labor or equipment, to circle around a neighbor in a crisis, to sell a heifer or lease a bull, to help out a new widow, to see that a kid got to go to college. Politics, too—usually despair about the latest Farm Bill.

Eventually Will saw that the men were also quietly watching out for Mamie, especially as she got older—no easy task, helping a woman with huge pride who in fact could do just about anything a man could do. She could string barbed wire fences alone, by attaching a cable come-along to her truck. She had good equipment. Her Powder River cattle chute and squeeze had an automatic head-catcher, which meant she could do most of her veterinary work herself, including pregnancy testing. What she liked best, though, was helping work a neighbor's cattle one day, then accept his help working hers the next.

What he heard from his perch on a stack of dog food bags near the saddle display was dominated by one subject: the weather. "How much rain did you get?" "Not enough." It was never enough. "Maybe six-tenths. And you?" If the other guy had gotten more, he would never say so, only something like "Just a sprinkle. The usual." Even when they didn't talk about rain, weather was almost always at the heart of it, that and the economy, the two things they couldn't control: whether they should dry plant or not, whether they would make enough hay for the winter without buying any, whether the new corn or soy bean hybrids might be more weather-resistant, whether they should spray this year, the high price of equipment, the falling prices of grain crops (down to half what they were in the fifties).

Hearing these stories at the feed and seed had helped turn Will Evans toward filmmaking. That is why he was making his way this particular Saturday morning to the local feed-and-seed store in a small town in rural upstate New York.

From the moment Will received the first letter from Socrates Tsinakis about filming, he imagined only one person for the role of Oedipus. There was one man in the business who had the voice, the range, the personal presence, and the depth of lived experience to make it work.

James Earl Jones.

Will called Jones's agent. Her answer, "No," came immediately. By way of explanation she added that Jones was not traveling much anymore and certainly would not be interested in going to Turkey for such a strenuous role.

Interventions from Hollywood friends led nowhere, and a message to the agent from Jones's old friend Gil Manning, maybe the best assistant director in the business, yielded the same negative answer. The only thing for Will to do was what Mamie always advised: If you want to get something done, go to the top.

232

Will journeyed to upstate New York where he knew Jones had a farm and figured he was likely to come into town to the Co-op on Monday morning, his day off from the play he was acting in on Broadway.

Will knew he had only one shot at it. It had to work the first time. He already had in mind, generally, what he would say, but he was nervous. It helped to remember how Telemachus in the *Odyssey*—strange how these snippets come back when you need them—gathered confidence on his way to call on Nestor for news about his father. "What will I say to him without seeming impertinent?" the boy asked the family friend Mentor, really Athena in disguise. Mentor's reply rang in Will's ears: "Your own intelligence and spirit will give you the words."

As Will expected, there he was, standing in the Co-op's row of power tools, that imposing man absolutely focused on a decision between two kinds of electric drills. Will took a slow deep breath. He had decided to say it all at once: "Mr. Jones, my name is Will Evans and I'm directing a joint Greek and Turkish production of *Oedipus at Colonus* for PBS next April at Ephesus, and you are the only person in the world who should play Oedipus and I want to ask you to do it."

Jones did not move. He lifted his eyes and stared at the wall in front of him. Then slowly he put down both drills, turning toward Evans in one massive motion. The men were the same height, but Will had to imagine steel cleats in his shoes to hold his ground.

"How dare you come to me here," he said in his familiar voice so low and deep you could sink in it and be grateful for the privilege.

Jones was furious. He glared menacingly with those eyes that could be any color of the sky. At this moment they were steel gray-blue.

233

Will narrowed his own gaze and answered slowly: "Because most men never get a chance to rehearse their own death."

Jones knew Sophocles' last play, knew it was about conflict between fathers and sons. The old story. His old story—his father, his son, both also actors sharing secret dramas among all three. Knew, too, of Oedipus's strange and luminous end, somehow redemptive after a lifetime of incalculable suffering.

The Purina clock on the wall seemed to stop. The other customers and clerks froze into a sepia daguerreotype. Long moments passed in which no one breathed. They carefully protected Jones's anonymity and were appalled at the audacity of this intruder.

Jones did not bellow. He did not shake the fist he had clinched when he heard the voice beside him. He did not smile either. He simply growled, "Call my agent one more time." And turned back to pondering the drills.

As Will reached the door, Jones turned half-way around. "If this is a Greek-Turkish thing, you might want to get in touch with Theodorakis and Livaneli about the music. They've been performing together."

* * *

In Ephesus Anne and Assistant Director Gil Manning made a point of having a meal together when they could. They liked each other and shared wide interests in politics and the arts. When they differed on how to handle some facet of the production, enough animated sparring usually brought them to common ground.

Manning was brought up the hard way in the Brownsville section of Brooklyn. He was a dreamer, and as a child he suffered acutely when he was left out of the neighborhood children's games. In time, however, he discovered a world more colorful and populous than even his vivid imagination could conceive.

As he finished high school and won a scholarship to Penn State, Gil kept thinking about that little camera Ben Shahn carried with him everywhere. He came to understand that painters could not do what photographers could. Neither could writers. As a child Gil loved to read and imagined becoming a writer, but in truth he didn't have the patience for it. He was a born extrovert, getting his energy from being around people, not from being alone. The camera—for him that would mean a movie camera—was just the right fast-action medium for his temperament.

One day Anne took Gil to eat at a place pointed out by a taxi driver. It was not a restaurant in any formal sense. It had no name and was located off a dirt road in the flat agricultural plain below the theater. The structure looked provisional, like something nomads would set up—open air, with a tent roof stretched over a wooden frame. Low Turkish benches surrounded the sides, covered with colorful hand-loomed pillows. Three crones sat on low stools in the middle, working wordlessly at their tasks. One mixed and kneaded dough, eventually working it into a ball the size of a large egg. Another chopped eggplants, onions, spinach, and roasted-lamb meat. A third expertly rolled the dough with a long thin wooden dowel into a flat circle more than two feet in diameter.

By that time Anne had learned enough Turkish words to place their order: spinach and meat for Gil, eggplant and onions for herself. The woman rolling the dough spread the ingredients in the center, then folded the sides into a flat rectangle about eight by fourteen inches. Lifting this over the center of her roller, she handed the dowel to a fourth, younger woman who had been tending the fire with sticks in an open stone fireplace domed into a chimney. She laid the rectangle down on the iron surface above the fire and toasted it quickly on each side. When it was ready, she handed it back to the third woman who chopped it with a large heavy knife into about six pieces. A young boy brought the plates over to the low table, together with a bottled soft drink. Anne and Gil mused that people had been cooking this way for thousands of years. It was delicious.

Today, Anne asked Gil how he got into the business. She already knew he had been the first assistant director on *Breakfast at Tiffany's* and the first *Godfather*. She had loved hearing him regale the crew with stories about how they brightened the lights on the wedding scene in the garden while lowering them into chiaroscuro in the godfather's study. And how they had to pay whole sets of Teamsters to look after each of the antique cars used in the film. And how Coppola insisted that only real Italians populate the wedding scene and that the wine and beer and food all be real Italian fare.

Gil continued: "You start with an immediate, observed event. Then you elaborate by making a real or imagined story around it. For example, you overhear a waiter in a bar say to a co-worker, 'I got my card today,' and you start thinking about his rebel parents dead in the armed struggle in some Central American country and his older brother coming to the U.S. and becoming a citizen and joining the Army and sending money home to his little brother to make sure he stayed in school until he could come to the U.S. too and work in a restaurant until he could get his card and perfect his English and get a better job and buy electronics and eventually a car and become a citizen and vote Republican."

Anne demanded: "How much of that did you make up just this minute?"

"None of it, except maybe the last part," Gil said.

"How did you know all that?" she asked.

"I asked him," he said.

"Oh," she said.

"But I could have made it all up. That would have been all right, too."

Anne thought silently for a moment. "But how did you get into film production?"

The nostalgia and affection in Gil's voice were palpable. "My brother Don. He was three years older." He stopped, caught his composure, then continued. "Don was a terrifically gifted designer. In the 1940s Jo Milziner was doing sets for all the great Broadway musicals—*Annie Get Your Gun; Kiss Me, Kate; Carousel;* all the rest. He taught set design classes at Cooper Union. We didn't have any money then, but Don took the entrance exam and got in.

Milziner took note of Don's gifts in one of his classes and asked him to join his staff. Later Don started his own scenic design company, doing television dramas for Playhouse 90, Philco Television Playhouse, and the like. I joined his company to do production work for his design projects. We had quite a run. Hardly ever disagreed on anything. Our temperaments were quite different, though. He was quiet, creative, artistic. I was often the tough guy for both of us. It worked out just fine."

There it is again, Anne thought. The old story. The sibling story.

Anne told Gil she would soon be going the next weekend to Athens for a short visit. "My father is there now with my sister Serena," she continued, "and I'd like to be there with them. My father has always wanted to see the Parthenon. His eyesight is failing now, but he got there in time."

Gil asked, "Tell me about your father. I know he lives in Santa Fe, but how did he get there?"

Anne felt his kindness lift her up. Here was someone else who wanted to know what was closest to her heart. Will already knew.

"His name is Clay Edwards. Dad always loved politics and is good at it. He can move around a room with a warm attentiveness that makes everyone feel valuable. He inherited a large ranch north of Amarillo and knows how to do everything on it—but, unlike many Texas men, he also loves art and music.

"Dad and my mother, Joanna Ware, married right out of college. He told her he was gay before they got engaged, but she badly wanted the position in the community he could give her. To be fair to her, she may have thought she could change him. And he badly wanted children, so it worked for a while.

"First Dad was elected mayor of Amarillo. He did a terrific job, even though there was constant controversy around the Pantex plant outside of town where most of the warheads for America's nuclear arsenal are assembled. Then he was elected president of the Texas Conference of Mayors and was able to bring that diverse group together for a few common endeavors. Soon after that, he was elected president of the U.S. Conference of Mayors.

"Their annual meeting was held in Kansas City. Serena and I went to support him and to hear his presidential address. He spoke about the importance of cities for our common lives, how they teach us to live together with others who are different from us. Cities, he said, protect private life and promote public life. Though public and private concerns often seem to conflict, it is the two together that make us human. Then, he said to those mayors: 'We are stewards of a legacy that came to us through the long labor of others and that we will pass on to those to come. Remember that our cities are in our trust—but only for a while.'

"Dad had told Serena and me two years earlier that he is HIV positive. That broke our hearts because we know what is coming. But we did not anticipate how he would conclude his speech.

"'I would like to end on a personal note. Folks, I am gay and I have AIDS. I am going to die from it. I am not happy about that. But I implore you to do two things. First, educate the young.

238

AIDS is so easily avoided and so fatal if it is not. Second, have compassion for those in your communities who are already suffering from this dreadful disease.' Then he sat down.

"No one moved. The silence was feeable. Then, a few people stood. Others joined them. The applause, a smattering at first, began to grow. Not everyone stood and applauded, but most did, tears in their eyes. Serena and I felt in that room that day a slight shift in the tide of history.

"Dad and Richard met through Dad's love of opera. From the beginning, each knew the other was the love of his life. They both had long been drawn by the magic of Santa Fe, so that's where they settled."

Gil sat quietly for a moment.

Then he said, "Anne, would you like me to go with you to Athens? It would be an honor to meet your father."

"That would be lovely," Anne said. "Thank you." At that moment she felt the troubled place in her soul settling a little.

Then Gil asked, "And your siblings? Will said you have two older brothers."

"Yes," said Anne. "Paul and Steve. Paul is the oldest. You might say he has spent his life in the big brother business. Steve is younger, an entrepreneur who loves making money."

Gil waited for more details, so Anne continued. "Both are very smart but so different that they have been in conflict all their lives. Now they are fighting for control of the family finances after Dad dies. And each is passionately righteous about his aspirations. Paul, who seems always to be competing with God, is determined to fund and control what he calls his 'Christian Institute for Public Policy.' He still lives in Amarillo. Steve is in Houston. His passion is investing in some new scheme for extracting oil from shale."

Anne thought for a moment. "Both of them seem to forget they have two sisters. They always have."

She did not add that she had just heard from a friend that Paul was threatening to come to Athens to try to bully his father into naming him sole executor.

Then, after a pause, Gil asked: "What about your mother?"

It was the question Anne always dreaded. She lowered her gaze. Sound stopped. The stork in her nest high above them sat motionless. Even the women at their cooking fires glanced toward her.

Without looking at Gil, she said in a low voice, "After our father came out at the meeting in Kansas City, she committed suicide."

* * *

One afternoon, leaving Gil to iron out some wrinkles between the Turkish and Greek crew members, Will and Anne went to see the Hanging Houses of Ephesus, sometimes called the Terrace Houses. They were in a fragile state of reconstruction, and the crowds of tourists were not allowed to visit them. A kindly curator had agreed to show them through.

In one of the rooms they were surprised to see a fresco depiction of a scene from a play of Euripides. Will commented, "Amazing how these plays persist, even here. Why is that?"

Anne had an answer, honed over the years because she had been asked the question by students so many times. "It's because they start where all good stories start, with the family drama. We recognize ourselves in them. But of course, one reason we know what we do about families is because we learned it from these Greek plays."

After a while they started back, passing the imposing Library of Celsus. Anne was wearing a coral cotton sundress and taupe linen espadrilles, together with jute-covered rubber soles and wraparound laces. Across from the commercial agora, a rough

240

pebble worked its way into her shoe. As Anne slowed and sat down to untie the laces, Will was already kneeling on the pavement in front of her. He took her hands, placed them on top of the other on her crossed knee, and reached behind her ankle to untie the laces. After he loosened the knot, he slowly unwrapped the crisscrossed laces, removed the shoe and placed it on the pavement. Then he took Anne's foot in both hands and, starting at the ankle, followed it with a firm and gentle pressure in one slow, smooth motion over her heel, arch, metatarsal, and toes. Then he replaced and tied the shoe.

For a moment the old haze of eros hovered between them. Soon it rose and wafted gently toward the blue Aegean. Anne and Will looked at each other and smiled. It had taken awhile, but by then they both knew that the true use of Greek tragedy is to help us keep from repeating it.

They rose, joined hands, and chatted happily all the way back to the theater.

Later that night Will, Gil, and Anne sat by the pool at the Kalehan after a frustrating day dealing with the Austrian archaeologists in charge of the theater. The bottle of Glenlivet on the table was going down at a steady clip.

Will never realized how much he missed having a mentor until he found one in Gil Manning. By mentor he did not mean an ego-driven superior trying to fashion a replica of himself. What he found in Gil was something much more accidental, a chance gift of recognition between two kindred souls at different stages of their careers. Their relationship was marked by an odd courtesy, a respect for difference, that left plenty of room for disagreement and even an occasional heated argument.

Will asked, "Tell me everything you know about filmmaking."

Manning was uncharacteristically silent for a long moment. "I can't do that. Wouldn't if I could. But I can't. It's art, don't you see? You can only do it out of who you are.

"What I *can* do is tell you what I learned, mostly indirectly, from Ben Shahn about it. Critics in the thirties and even later tried to make Shahn into a 'cinematic' photographer. I don't think he thought of himself that way. He didn't often make his photographs into a narrative series. But he was fascinated with the street as a living theater.

"He scorned the elite art establishment's pride in 'disengagement' as essential for artistic creation. That's why Ben was intrigued with movies, which he saw as combining photographs and painting—the direct connection, the immediate snapshot of real life—'social realism' some called it—together with a more reflective, intentional, or composed interpretation.

"Ben started with the 'living theater' of the streets and made art from there. That's what Greek theater is. In an interview in 1965 he said, 'If I could do it again, I would have gone into movies.' He thought cinema has everything: image, music, speech—total communication."

Anne added quietly: "It's about stories. It always is."

"Now," said Manning, "I'll put it my way. Know yourself. Film what you know, which means what you love. Get started. Keep going. Keep growing. Never repeat yourself.

"That's about all I know to say. That, and surround yourself with the best people you can find."

In the dark none saw the other two nod in agreement.

Will thought about how grateful he was for the life he had chosen and was able to lead—for filmmaking, for Mamie, for Emile, and for his other friends. And now for Gil and Anne—friends for the duration. A tripod, the most stable structure of all.

In that moment, six thousand miles and two continents away, everything Will Evans was grateful for seemed as fine and clear as a boundless Texas sky.

Penelope Returning

Alone on the shore of Ithaca, Penelope sat
absorbed in the shimmer of the dusk-bronzed sea,
searching for ways to tell what happened
after Odysseus came home at last.

Once he had powered his way into
his rightful place with his great bow,
she loosed the string of hers,
her vigil done, her only child now launched

beyond the reach of his mother's kind eyes
hiding the worries that circled her counsel
throughout his life, the two decades she
leaned toward him with all her weight and wit.

She conceived her plan a year after Odysseus's return,
waited patiently until the time was right.
Mentes arrived to rest his merchant crew,
take provisions, visit Ithaca for the night.

In early morning upon their olive bed
she turned quietly to Odysseus and said:
"I'll go to Egypt now. I've always wanted to.
Mentes will take me. I'll be safe, I know."

Her husband swung his gaze toward her,
mind churning with all the habits of manhood
the world and his birth had prescribed,

once again caught by the force of her courage.

Odysseus had loved her first for her beauty,
hard thereafter for her far-arching heart,
soon upon that for her competence,
the gift that promises a partnership for life.

"Yes," he nodded, "of course." He knew his wife.
She gathered what she needed for the journey,
and then put at least half of it away.
Half her joy the thought of traveling light.

She prepared a feast for the evening meal,
embraced the household, turned with a heavy heart
and steady step to board the craft
that would give her to the world.

As they rounded the western shoals
of Cephalonia she began to sense
what she had done. Demons of doubt
raised their frenzied whirl around her.

Guilt eroded her resolve. She wept
inconsolably, salt tears mixed with spray
at the stern where she fixed her eyes back
toward the home she left with such apparent ease.

She cried without trying to stop, only later
identifying guilt as the first monster
she must face and overcome. Others loomed
as soon as she pondered all she left behind:

How would father and son get along in her absence,
still new to each other and so little together,
son learning to become a man,
Odysseus at last learning to father?

Would they eat meals at tables
laced with thought and conversation,
or merely feed their hunger grazing
as they passed the cooking fires?

A serving girl, Melantho's daughter,
shifty-eyed and waitful, watched her depart;
Penelope saw her calculating her chances
with the master while the mistress was away.

Then, as the ship split the gentling waves
into the open sea, a moment came, still
as a hummingbird suspended, when she felt
duty fade and the joy of solitude encircle her

like the lifting light shining around
a well-loved child in love with life,
but burnished now far brighter by all
she knew from all the living she had earned.

Turning confident toward the bow, she did not
again look back. She reached Egypt,
climbed the pyramids as she had dreamed,
ate alone at dusk, made strange new friends.

No suitors waited slaying on her arrival home,
for she had razed hers one by one upon the road.

Like a sphinx, she left their leers in the markets
leveled with lances from her steely gaze.

With one like-minded journeyer she shared a meal;
every story sparked another, flint for one another's steel.
They parted with regret, braced only by guessing
how great the love at home that taught each how to love.

Still he is lodged in her heart's estate
that no heir will ever know,
nor gaggle of glaring shrews who confuse
their envy with their rectitude.

She is home. To most she seems the same,
though the sun's magic has settled on her skin,
her hair gleams free as a dancing child's,
turquoise eyes ashine with something new.

For a while she is strangely lonely,
chooses selectively the duties she resumes,
finds it hard to become host of her own home again
after being so long a guest of the world.

She delights to give the gleaming gifts
chosen so carefully for her beloveds,
sorrowing only that she must meter the density
of detail of how she came upon each prize.

She rises, returns to the hearth of her heart's content,
knows at last that Ithaca is not the journey
but the catalog of stories
to make the journey known.